Darkness and Spice

Darkness and Spice

JUNIPER HARTMANN

Table of Contents

Playlist

CLOSER

Nine Inch Nails

RULE #34

Fish in a Birdcage

HOLY SMOKES

Bohnes

STRIPPED

Shiny Toy Guns

FLESH

Simon Curtis

ANIMALS

Maroon 5

HATEF--K

The Bravery

THE CULT OF DIONYSUS

The Orion Experience

REV 22:20

Puscifer

Disclaimer

This collection contains extremely
graphic, and often offensive material.

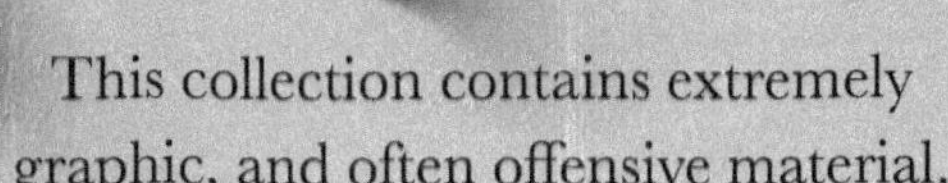

You will find kinks and trigger warnings
before every short for your convenience.

Feel free to skip anything that doesn't
suit your fancy! That's the beauty of
these stories- you can read whatever you
like and leave the rest behind!

IT IS ALSO IMPORTANT TO
NOTE THAT THESE ARE BDSM
FANTASIES. THEY ARE NOT
INTENDED FOR EDUCATION.

for *every* person who just wants
to feel desire without shame

you are not wrong for your desires

Make Me Cry

Caroline returns from a long day at work,
stressed to her brink and ready to unwind.
Luckily for her, Sarrah knows just the trick.

PAIRING:

FF

KINKS INCLUDED:

Forced Orgasms, Restraint System,
Soft Topping

SPICE LEVEL:

1/10

CHARACTERS:

Caroline, Sarah

CAROLINE

As soon as the clock struck 5:00, Caroline leaped from her seat. The bustle of her coworkers readying to leave filled what had been moments ago an eerie, stretching silence. While she was thankful for her corporate salary and the ability to take care of her disabled wife, the robotic corporate environment made her shudder. Only the warm touch of her darling Sarah could thaw the chill that called her bones home.

They had plans tonight. That was why she was in such a rush.

Her redbacks clacked smartly on the marble floors. Sarah loved her business wear, said it made her look every bit like the femme she was.

Sarah was different altogether. She was more of the garden variety… literally so. The best days of Sarah's life were spent among plants, tending to their needs and nurturing them from little sprouts to towering monsters thick with luscious growth.

It had been her gentle heart and warm demeanor that had attracted Caroline. She loved the way that Sarah could venture out into the woods with nothing but wine and a hammock, and be entirely at peace doing it.

It was the free spirit and dreamer that Caroline had fallen in love with. That was the X at the end of the trail she was always meant to find. It would always come down to Sarah for her.

SARAH

Sarah was biting her nails again. If Caroline had been home, she would have been deeply disappointed. Sarah pulled her hand away from her mouth and heaved a sigh, her eyes snapping to the smartwatch clinging tightly to her wrist.

Her wife would be home soon. Sarah's heart skipped a beat.

Their room was prepared. The candles had been lit for hours, allowing their musky scent to richly perfume the air. Teakwood and mahogany, Caroline's favorite, were thick in every breath. Sarah had spared no expense and left no detail disregarded. Every bit of her day had been spent perfecting the scene where they'd make love that night.

It was like the first time every single time. She would never get over the soft curve of Caroline's jerking hips as she came, the animalistic cry that would rip from her throat. She could make all of it happen with nothing but her fingers and mouth. There was something so erotic in that; she could bring Caroline such intense pleasure with those simple tools alone.

She heard the door open, jerking her from her thoughts. Caroline was home.

CAROLINE

It was unusually quiet when she stepped into their

apartment. There was a faint scent in the air, smokey and alluring. Caroline's bright red lips popped open into a small smile. Warmth surged in her lower belly as a pulse beat steadily between her legs.

Caroline didn't bother hanging up her bag, dumping it unceremoniously onto the floor. She kicked off the heels and padded quickly down the hallway. Portraits of their travels lined the walls, memories from adventures around the world. Even though their interests diverged so drastically, they did intensely share the love of *experiences.*

Plus, she got to see Sarah in nothing but a flimsy bikini whenever they weren't tangled up in the sheets. It was a sight to behold–the thick, lengthy legs that led to gently sloping hips, her love handles plump around the straps. Caroline wanted nothing more in those moments than to wrap her hands around those hips and pull her close. She craved every curve of her body… and was sorely hoping to find them on display when she walked in.

She shed her clothing slowly. The cherry red blazer slipped from her shoulders. Next, she worked the buttons of the crisp linen tank top beneath it. Once the white shirt fell open at the front, she began taking out her earrings.

Caroline gave a shaky sigh before she turned the corner into their room. She always felt a strange shame whenever she had the chance to show her love sincerely and intimately. The same worries flitted through her mind like scenes from a projector.

What if she couldn't please her?

What if Sarah secretly couldn't stand their sex life?

What if she was only pretending to fall to pieces beneath her ministrations?

But as soon as she laid eyes on their bed, every thought evaporated.

SARAH

Sarah was lying on her side, outfitted in salacious lingerie, all white and lace and silk. The bright panties and bra stood out in contrast to her deep bronze skin. She knew she looked like an angel…

But she would prove to be the devil she was before the night was over.

Daisy petals topped their black comforter. On the side table, she had placed a bottle of their favorite wine and a platter of goodies—chocolate-covered strawberries, pretzels with honey mustard dip, grapes on the vine, and whipped cream.

Caroline looked exhausted. Her long hair had come loose from the professional bun she'd wrapped it into before work, and her shirt hung open. She was just standing there, slack-jawed.

"Baby, come here," Sarah whispered, holding out her hand. Still wrapped up in the spell cast by her lover's looks, Caroline started forward, eyes shining with anticipation. The bed sunk slightly as she joined her.

Sarah wasted no time in leaning forward, pressing

her mouth into Caroline's, her hand gently cupping her wife's face. Parted lips let their tongues slip into each other's mouths as the kiss deepened. There was a soft moan, but Sarah wasn't sure who it came from.

She pulled back, but stayed close enough for their foreheads to touch. For a moment, all she did was breathe in the gentle waft of perfume lifting from Caroline's neck. It was powdery and incredibly soft. Caroline said she liked it because it reminded her of Sarah.

Those little confessions made her heart stop.

"I got some toys out," Sarah said, biting her lip to hold back a grin. Normally, Caroline would lay Sarah back and worship her body until she was in tatters. Tonight?

Tonight was all about Caroline.

Sarah knew she was struggling with her workload, stressed to her breaking point, and in dire need of something to take her mind off it all. She knew just the thing to perk her back up.

"I like the sound of that."

The response stirred a hot desire in Sarah's core as wetness gathered. She wouldn't be surprised if there was a noticeable dark spot in the middle of her panties. It was what Caroline always managed to do to her with nothing but a kiss.

"Why don't you slip into something more comfortable, sweetheart? Preferably nothing at all," The sultry purr that pulled Caroline closer, lips brushing gently against Sarah's.

"Anything you want, my love."

Sarah watched in rapt attention as Caroline stood to slip her work clothing off. Every movement outlined the sweeping curves and slopes she desperately wanted to cover with her mouth. When Caroline's bra dropped to the floor, Sarah sucked in a sharp breath. She was forever insatiable for this incredible woman.

CAROLINE

As soon as her clothing hit the floor, Sarah was upon her with soft, manicured hands. She gently guided her to lay back against the pile of pillows meticulously organized to provide an extravagant experience to her lover.

Sarah uncorked the wine and expertly poured two glasses. She handed one to Caroline, taking a sip from hers and smiling over the rim. She was seated on the end of the bed, one leg crooked beneath her while the other hung off the edge.

"Come here," Caroline said with a laugh, leaning up from her soft throne to wrap an arm around Sarah's waist. Sarah shimmied away, her butt popping off the bed, and almost fell over completely.

"Oh, careful!"

Caroline dissolved into giggles, grabbing Sarah's hand to keep her seated. A little wine had sloshed onto Sarah's neck, leaving a red line trailing down onto her breasts. Caroline's heartbeat pumped harder as she leaned forward.

"Here, let me take care of that." She wrapped her whisper around Sarah like a rope. Caroline leaned forward and ran her tongue from between the cleft of her chest up to her ear, taking a lobe in her mouth and sucking.

A hitching moan escaped Sarah.

"No, stop it," she said, pushing Caroline back into the nest of pillows, "This is about you, my love. Just lay back and let me do the work."

"Alright, fine. You don't make it easy. God, I want to taste you…" Her eyes were wine-bright even through the lust glazing them. Caroline felt her pussy quiver.

Sarah gently fed her wife, Caroline's lips parting to accept offerings of grapes, cheese, and strawberries. Then came the whipped cream. Her heart skipped a beat.

"And what do you plan on doing with that?" she questioned with an arched brow.

"Eat it, dummy. But I am awful clumsy, aren't I?" She shook the can and squeezed a line down Caroline's stomach, "See? Oops!"

Caroline couldn't help but laugh as she leaned back, but it was lost into a moan as Sarah's tongue drew a line up her torso, making good on her promise to taste the trail she'd sprayed. *God*, it felt incredible. Caroline whimpered and shook as Sarah tasted her with whisper-light touches and answering moans.

When she leaned up and gathered her hair into a ponytail, Caroline knew.

Her head fell back, eyes closing as her legs tensed in anticipation.

"Are you ready?" she whispered. Caroline gulped, head foggy with desire. She managed to whisper that she was, and let Sarah spread her legs wide. Her wife laid between her thighs, wrapping her arms under them and pulling them tight around her head. Sarah adored the way Caroline would squeeze all of her muscles, making her pleasure known.

With a few wet kisses to Caroline's pussy lips, her worship began.

SARAH

The first taste sent shockwaves through her system. Sarah rolled her eyes back and groaned, tongue sliding up Caroline's slick slit. Caroline was absolutely *dripping*. The familiar tang hit her tongue and she threw herself into it, desperate for more of the ambrosia that flowed from her wife's pussy.

Focusing most of her attention on Caroline's swollen clit, she brought her fingers into the game earlier than she usually did. Sarah loved making her wife come with nothing but her tongue. It was one of life's simple pleasures and a confirmation of her abilities.

She let her index and pointer fingers slide deep into her wife's velvety pussy, immediately crooking them at the first knuckle. Caroline let out a howl, her thighs clenching and back arching.

"That's it, baby, come for me," she growled, revealing the primal side that Caroline so loved. Keeping a steady rhythm with her fingers, she went back to swirling her tongue around the tiny nub that would push her over the edge. When she covered it with her lips and began sucking, Caroline gasped for breath.

"Oh, God, fuck," she was babbling through her orgasm, and it was music to Sarah's ears. Her face was covered in her lover's passion, and her head spun as she tried to sate her appetite. It never worked. She would be ravenous again by morning, when the sunbeams through their gauzy curtains hit Caroline's face just right.

She pulled back and was immediately met with Caroline's objecting whimpers.

"Hold on, baby," Sarah crooned, running a finger down Caroline's thick thigh.

It was time for the next portion of their night. There were only so many times Caroline could come before it would be too much…

And Sarah intended to take her far, far beyond that limit. She had already set up the scene, and her wife had no idea.

She slipped off the bed and grabbed a strap hanging from the bedpost. Pulling it over to Caroline, she set down the end with the comfortable cuff.

"Oh, we really are pulling out all the stops," Caroline said, eyeing the restraint with obvious hesitation. It wasn't real, just a game they played to spice things up before she would give in and let Sarah push her limits.

"Absolutely, we are."

Sarah made quick work of cuffing all of Caroline's limbs, pulling the straps tight so that she was spread-eagle, although not so stretched that it would be uncomfortable. With shaking hands, she pulled a large, velvet box out from under the bed.

This should do nicely, she thought, picking out a vibrating dildo and a clitoral suction toy. She knew exactly how to get her wife to where she wanted her—screaming out for mercy and writhing as she fought the restraints.

Placing the toys beside her wife's leg, she crawled up over her body and put her lips next to Caroline's ear.

"What do you need, baby? Use your words," she whispered.

"Please. I need you to make me cry." The whine was underscored by a whimper.

Sarah smiled in response, drawing back and staring down at her wide-eyed, wild-haired wife. She was absolutely dazzling. This was when Sarah loved her most.

The air crackled with electricity as the wait began. Sarah smeared a little bit of tingling lube on Caroline's clit, reveling in the noises she made.

CAROLINE

She felt Sarah's cool fingers rubbing the slick liquid into that bundle of nerves that would betray her over and over again in the coming hour… hours? She was never sure how long things lasted. It all became a blur after a while.

But she was exhausted. She felt the hunger for slumber settling deep in her bones. She wouldn't last long, and she knew that Sarah would be mindful of that. Even so, she wondered how far they could take it before she finally broke.

"Okay, baby, get ready," were the last words she heard before the vibrator buzzed. Caroline sucked in a sharp breath as the clitoral sucker came down on her glistening mound.

"Holy shit, fuck, ah!" Caroline cried out, the expletives driven on by the uncontrollable, shuddering surges of pleasure wreaking havoc on her every nerve ending.

"That's it. Just give in, baby, I'm here," Sarah said, leaning up to lock her lips onto Caroline's. Their mouths gently brushed against each other as Caroline whimpered, pleading for more.

It always began like this. She would start out begging for a higher setting, to be filled, to be *fucked*. It would end with her crying for mercy and begging Sarah to stop. The rise and fall never failed to captivate her.

The entire way, Sarah was there to guide her. She may have been the gentlest soul Caroline had ever met, but that personality flipped once they were in the confines of their bedroom. The sheer glee in her eyes while Caroline struggled was as erotic as it was shocking.

Her hips quaked as Sarah tapped the vibrator up and down on her clit. It was delicious. It was horrible.

It was *everything she needed*. Her moans were long and low, filling the perfumed air. An incredible sense of release fell over her body as her orgasm hit.

Caroline gasped for breath as Sarah pulled the toy away. Her brows furrowed as she realized what was coming next.

She felt prodding at her entrance, a head sliding in and out, teasing her relentlessly. Caroline let out a frustrated wail and wiggled her hips helplessly. Sarah, seemingly unfazed, simply continued the slow drag–in and out, in and out. Caroline let out a cry as the entire length of the toy slid inside of her.

She felt Sarah twisting the knob at the base, and the dildo came alive inside of her with a heavy vibration she felt through her entire lower belly.

"Alright, baby, it's time," Sarah crooned, reaching up to brush Caroline's hair from her face.

"Please, oh God, I can't," she croaked out, panic rising as she realized she was entirely helpless and that this woman was obviously intent on seeing her sanity fade.

"You can, I promise. You can for me."

The vibrator came down on her clit again, and her back arched painfully off of the bed. The restraints kept her firmly in place. Sarah laid between her legs again and looped an arm around one of Caroline's legs so that her arm could act as a bar across her stomach, keeping her still.

Caroline cried out as she realized she was trapped. Her hips tried to buck, but Sarah was strong from years of volunteering at farms.

"Stop trying to get away from it, or I'll put you over my knee, darling," she crooned, tapping the vibrator again. Caroline's vision exploded into white and black and stars.

SARAH

She was coming completely undone. Sarah's own pussy was throbbing while she worshipped Caroline's. It was her greatest joy to watch her wife squirm and lose herself to the heady pleasure only Sarah could bring her. She would find her release after, by herself. Caroline would be too exhausted to return the favor.

That was okay with Sarah. It was fully her intention to put her wife to sleep.

The moans were building in volume and intensity, close to a fever pitch. Sarah knew the finale was almost upon them, and she squeezed her thighs together in anticipation. It was going to be delicious.

She watched in ecstasy as Caroline pulled at her restraints, eyes shut. Her mouth was contorted from the pleasure she felt. Sarah knew it must be coming in powerful, crushing waves at this point. It was time to shatter the dam entirely.

She leaned forward and captured one of Caroline's nipples in her mouth, rolling the peak with her tongue and sucking harshly. The hand that wasn't holding the vibrator came up to play with the other breast, softly rolling and squeezing and pulling.

"No, no, no, oh, no," Caroline groaned, throwing her head back. So close. She was *so* close that Sarah could practically feel it. Her nipple was perfectly pebbled between Sarah's fingers. She rolled the peak between her fingers, eliciting some of the sweetest noises she had ever heard. Sarah pulled back and put a hand between her wife's legs.

"Alright, baby, it's time," she said, raising her voice to overcome Caroline's plaintive mewling.

"No, wait, stop!"

The cry went unheeded. Sarah began thrusting the dildo, pressing the vibrator firmly into Caroline's clit. The love of her life was thrashing helplessly, screaming out, begging her to stop, that it was too much, that she *couldn't*.

"Yes, you can. Just let go, baby. I'm right here, it's okay."

With that, Caroline let loose entirely. Her screams became animalistic.

CAROLINE

The orgasm hit like a hurricane. The sharp, whipping pleasure was pushing her to a rising frenzy. Caroline had entirely lost control of her mouth, the words blurring together between pleading cries.

Mercy would not come. Caroline surely would, however.

The first wave died down, but was quickly replaced by a tsunami that threatened to drown her completely. Her mouth opened wide and she gagged and choked on her own moans, desperately fighting the restraints that kept her locked in place, unable to escape.

And then, there it was, the peak.

She was soaring somewhere high above herself, simultaneously entirely in the moment and absolutely out of body. The pleasure had turned almost to pain, sharp threads of it weaving through her womb and deep into her loins.

Her pussy was *rippling*.

And then there was a wetness on her face, a tickling sensation as the tears began to fall. She felt empty, a sensation that was welcome wholly, a reprieve from her racing mind.

Sarah pulled the toys away, tossing them to the floor. Caroline knew she'd dutifully clean them after. The restraints were released, and Caroline immediately pulled her limbs back in so that she was lying comfortably on her back.

There was a rubbing sensation, and she hissed as Sarah began cleaning her up. She was so sensitive between her legs that even the soft brush of a cloth sent her spiraling.

"I'm sorry, baby, but I can't let you go to bed like this," Sarah muttered her apology.

A soft kiss was placed on her throat as she felt her body sinking into slumber.

"You did so good for me. I love fucking you to sleep."

With that, Caroline drifted off, far lighter than she had been before.

The Spice of Life

Three friends find themselves in the same room and a strange predicament. Can Elle overcome her internalized shame and join in the fun?

PAIRING:

MFF

KINKS INCLUDED:

Couple/Friend, Sensory Deprivation, Ass
Play, Rough Handling, Alcohol Usage

SPICE LEVEL:

2/10

CHARACTERS:

Kate, Elle, Alex

They were both here to worship her.

Elle was mostly ignorant of the art of sexuality, but experimentation and inexperience were welcome in this dark, steamy space that had been made just for her.

Thick curtains hung in swooping lengths that gathered heavily on the floor. Everything around her was a shade of black, with highlights of red thrown in to further set the mood. Elle was still trying to figure out what *her* mood was.

Excited?

Thrilled?

Terrified?

Elle's limited number of previous partners had never put in this type of effort. It was astounding to her. She obviously didn't have the same mileage as the two people sitting in front of her, intently watching while they waited for a response.

"Mmm, I feel safe. Really safe, actually," she breathed out, feeling the familiar rush of blood that pinkened her cheeks. She felt comforted and cared for, but it was still hard to stare down something so blatantly sexual. She wasn't sure how she'd handle the actual scene.

"Are you sure, Elle? It's okay to say no," Alex said, reaching out a hand to touch hers.

"And if you feel unsafe at any point, you know the safe word, right?" Kate continued.

Elle sucked in a slow breath, breathing deep and low, before she answered.

"Let's do it."

DARKNESS & SPICE

***

Elle trembled as she pulled on the scant attire they had laid out for her on the four-poster bed. The ground was covered in a thick shag rug that felt luxurious beneath her mostly bare feet. There were pillows and a low table gathered into a little circle across from the bed.

She wondered how many of the props they were going to get to use.

There were cuffs on her wrists and ankles, all equipped for restraining her to any of the number of implements scattered around the room. Elle had requested they go all out; she wanted the *full* experience. No stone was to be left unturned in this uncovering of her deeper desires.

Kate was a stunner in sultry lingerie that complemented every long curve of her body. Elle had always been jealous of her figure, although looking back, it was likely that the jealousy was actually a giant crush she was hiding from. She didn't want to be Kate, she wanted to be *in* her.

The panties and bra were black as their surroundings and looked like silk, although Elle hadn't had the pleasure of testing this theory quite yet. She was allowed to look, but not to touch.

The thought made her heart clench. Her upbringing had told her this was wrong, but now, it was everything she wanted out of life. She yearned to feel the bite of a whip against her bare skin or the drag of a heel across her neck. A shiver shot down her spine at the thought.

She looked up as Alex approached, muscles rippling as he worked the rope in his hands. When he stopped mere inches away, hovering over her, she felt heat pool between her tensed thighs.

Here we go, she thought to herself, wondering whether she'd regret this, or if it would consume her entirely.

"Stand."

The command came on a low, husky breath. It left no room for argument. Elle obeyed almost on instinct, scrambling to rise. Even on her feet, he stood head and shoulders above her. Blood drained from her face, and her mouth dried when he gripped an arm and turned her around without warning.

A hand pressed against the middle of her back, guiding her toward the bed. She could feel the steady thrum of desire snaking through her system, coiling tightly in her belly. When they arrived at their destination, he pushed her over so that she was bent at the hips, hands out to brace against the bed.

Alex tangled his fingers in her hair, the other hand guiding her back into an arch, and he forced her head backward so that he could whisper into her ear.

"From this point forward, you are going to be our little fucktoy. We are going to use every single one of these holes in any way we wish."

He brushed his lips against her cheek, a moment of tenderness to reassure and cut the tension. Elle moaned lightly, lips parted and eyes squeezed shut. She wanted it so badly, but somehow it was more comfortable if she didn't have to see it.

As though summoned by her thoughts, Kate appeared next to Alex. She could barely see her thighs in her peripheral vision.

"This will make things so much more fun." A gentle croon came before a blindfold came into view. "Don't be embarrassed, Elle. There's nothing to be ashamed of."

Kate's voice was dripping like honey, thick and sultry. Elle felt her blood run hot in her veins. Every beat of her heart was punctuated by a throb at the apex of her thighs. She wanted Kate so badly that it hurt.

Elle lifted her head to help Kate place the blindfold. The comfort of darkness followed, and Elle's shoulders relaxed with the loss of her sight. Her breath came out as a hitching gasp when Kate's slender finger brushed against her jawline.

Alex was rubbing her ass, moving his hand slowly toward her pussy. She bucked her hips backward, a light, half-hearted movement born of inexperience. She didn't know what she was doing, but it seemed her body might.

Her plan was simply to follow along.

Alex's throaty chuckle filled the room, a low, gravelly voice following close behind, "So desperate to be our little slut, aren't you? I can't wait to feel that tight cunt wrapped around my cock."

Elle gasped. She'd only heard words like that from the mouths of filthy, leering men on the city streets. But now, coming from him, she practically melted under the attention. It was intoxicating. She *did* want to be their little slut. Desperately.

Abruptly, her head was yanked back, sending shooting pleasure and sharp pain ricocheting. Her mouth opened wide with an onslaught of sharp moans and pathetic pants. Elle fell back into Alex's bulky chest, an arm encircling her waist.

"I think we can get started," Kate said.

"Oh, absolutely. Where do we begin, though? So many choices..." Alex trailed off in thought.

She assumed they were using hand motions to discuss whatever delicious deviance they planned to inflict on her. It would ruin the surprise, after all, if they used their words. What was the point of the blindfold if she could see it coming?

They began guiding her, helping Elle navigate across the room. She loved the feeling of the thick, shag carpet poking through the holes in the fishnets. Elle couldn't help but feel so incredibly naughty wearing something so revealing.

"Sit down, darling," Kate said, helping her down to the pillows. She assumed this meant they were at the table. "You look so thirsty. How about a drink?"

"Please," Elle croaked. She hadn't realized how parched she was until now.

"Here. It's your favorite." Kate cupped her chin gently and held a bottle to her lips. Elle drank greedily, especially when she realized it was a light, crisp Mexican beer. The carbonation tickled her tongue as the beer went down her throat. It was delightfully smooth.

They really had thought of everything.

"Alright, that's enough," Kate giggled, scolding. "We don't want you to get tipsy."

Elle pouted as the bottle was removed, but then froze still as a frightened deer when she felt soft, plump lips cover her own. Instinctually, her mouth opened when she felt the prodding of an insistent tongue. When she felt Kate's tongue slide against hers, it was over. She dove into the kiss, pouring passion and intensity into every moment. When Kate pulled back, Elle was gasping for air.

"My turn, Kate," Alex said, and she felt his hand on her shoulder.

"Good. I have a better idea," Kate responded, breathless.

She felt lips descend on hers again, this time rougher and more demanding. Elle whimpered and responded in kind, feeling Kate's hands stroke her thighs. She squeezed them together before she could stop herself.

"Absolutely not, darling," Kate said, firm but kind. She pried Elle's knees open and placed a hand firmly on her core.

Elle felt like she was going to explode.

Hand in place, Kate allowed Elle to close her knees again. "I think we'll just get used to touch for now."

Soft noises began pushing up from her tightened throat. Between the desperate mouth covering her own, to the warm hand gently rubbing against her aching pussy, Elle was overwhelmed. Finally, Alex broke away, and she threw her head back and panted heavily.

"What a good girl for us," he crooned, running his hand through her hair. Elle realized she must look absolutely wild from being tossed around and kissed so thoroughly. The thought made her skin prickle.

"How about something to help keep her mind occupied?"

"Ooh, I like it. What do you have in mind?"

Then, silence. Elle's heart and mind raced against each other as she wondered what they had in store next. She shifted gently against the hand still cupping her. Kate resumed moving her hand. It was a gentle back and forth, a featherlight touch that made Elle drip and wriggle desperately for more.

"Why don't you open those legs, sweetheart?"

The sound of Kate's voice was soothing–low, and sweet. With a gulp, she obeyed, slowly spreading herself wide.

"I'm going to use my hands to make you feel good, okay?"

She couldn't bring herself to respond. The heat was searing. It couldn't be ignored. *God*, did she want this. Once she was entirely open to Kate, Elle let her head fall back again and focused on breathing. Not being able to see what was happening, she was forced to focus on the touch.

She felt fingers sliding inside of her through the fishnet's holes. They began stroking, crooked in a way that felt heavenly. Elle nearly shrieked in pleasure.

And then a mouth. *Her* mouth.

Kate's tongue found her clit almost immediately, and it sent Elle into spasms. She writhed, hips grinding into Kate's face. Pressure built steadily with each stroke of her fingers and brush of her tongue. Even with the stockings in the way, Kate seemed to expertly work around any obstacle.

"Tell us when you're close," Alex said, a sharp edge to his voice that said there would be consequences if she didn't.

Consequences.

The idea was so foreign and so wildly erotic that it almost sent her over the edge, until she remembered what he had commanded of her.

"I-I'm close," she stuttered out, chest heaving with the effort of holding back her orgasm. She wished she hadn't, because in the next moment, Kate pulled away entirely.

"You don't get to come until we let you," she heard Kate's voice explain. Elle wanted to argue. She wanted to talk back, to demand she finish the job, to tell them that this was bullshit.

She did nothing yet. She simply whimpered, and then said, "Okay."

There was silence for a few moments, before

Kate's giggle broke it. Goosebumps raised along her body as Elle waited for the next round.

"Turn over, darling. Lay on your stomach."

Without a second thought, Elle did as she was instructed. Maybe if she was a very good girl, they'd let her come soon. She wasn't sure what the requirements were for unlocking her release, but she was anxious to meet them.

She folded her arms and rested her head on them, trying to relax as best she could under the circumstances. They'd said they were going to use *all* of her holes. It hadn't quite struck her until now. They'd discussed beforehand what she was okay with. Anal was on the table.

Cool lube hit her ass, making her jump a little. Alex and Kate both laughed softly, and she thought it was Alex who slipped his lubed fingers between her ass cheeks. The hands were too large and rough to belong to Kate.

In the next moment, she felt Kate's softer hand stroke her face, and she knew that she'd been right.

"Just relax, sweetheart. It's going to feel so good."

Elle had every reason to believe her. This warm, lovely human could be trusted. Of that, she was sure.

When his fingers began prodding at the entrance between those spread cheeks, Elle bit her lip. She wasn't a huge fan of the process of getting the toy inside of her, but the pleasure afterward was worth a small amount of pain. She'd done as they'd instructed and practiced by herself, but it always pinched fiercely when sliding in.

Kate knew this, and she would comfort her through the process.

She felt a finger slide in and she gasped. Her body tensed on reflex. Kate whispered something she couldn't quite hear and then left her side. She was back quickly, promising Elle that this would make things easier.

She quickly found out that *this* was a little vibrator.

"Lift your hips, love," Kate said, easing her hand between Elle's torso and the carpet. She did as she was told, and a loud buzz sounded in the silent room. Elle groaned into her folded arms. She'd moved up to her knees, bent over at the hips, back arched.

Elle felt the toy press into her clit and moaned shamelessly, her cries of pleasure overpowering the motor of the toy that worked tirelessly against her clit.

"That's it, baby girl, just like that," Alex said, increasing to two fingers, pumping his hand steadily. He was stretching her slowly, but the pressure was still *so close* to overwhelming her.

With the vibrator in the mix, it nearly did. She was shipless in a tossing ocean that showed neither mercy nor signs of slowing. Whether her hips shifted up or down, there was pressure one way or the other. Either she could press herself into the incessant vibrations, or push herself further onto Alex's twisting fingers.

She felt that familiar heat building in her belly and she called out, "I'm close."

This time, her voice was confident and steady, faltering only with the sheer ecstasy flowing through her.

Kate pulled the vibrator away, leaning down to kiss Elle's cheek.

"Good girl," she breathed into her ear.

Elle swelled with something entirely unfamiliar at the words, something like satisfaction. With a start, Elle realized that it pleased her deeply to earn the praise of her—what? Masters? Perhaps that was something they could explore next time. *Next time?* Would there be one? She hoped there was, desperately so.

Alex removed his fingers. "I'm going to fuck that pretty little ass now, Elle."

She whimpered. She couldn't bring herself to verbalize beyond moans and grunts. It was humiliating in the best way. When he ripped open the back of her fishnets, another string of wordless noise fell out of her mouth.

The head of his cock pushed at her back entrance. She felt herself stretching to accommodate his girth, and she hissed. Kate was back, stroking her face as she whispered affirmations in her ear.

"Okay, darling, I'm going to get into position now. You're going to use that lovely mouth of yours on me. I like my clit sucked the most, so focus on that. Don't forget to use your fingers. You won't be allowed to get off unless you can get me off first."

Elle had plenty of questions, but she choked on all of them when Alex began pushing himself further in. She groaned, shifting side to side as he filled her ass. Once she could feel his hips pressed against her cheeks, she knew he was buried all the way in.

All eight inches of him. She couldn't breathe.

And then it hit her: she was expected to eat this other woman out.

Elle had never done that before. If things got too intense, she could always use the safe word. She didn't want to, though. She wanted to know what Kate tasted like, wanted to feel her soft pussy quiver under her twisting tongue.

She felt Kate slide underneath her, and she knew that if she ducked her head down, she would breathe in that beautiful scent.

"Don't be shy, Elle. Go on," Alex grunted out as he drove into her in short, harsh bursts. Elle groaned under the strain of accepting him, but she put her head down. She was quickly rewarded by the feeling of coarse hair under her nose. Pushing down, she found the slick slit. Her tongue slipped from her mouth and she began working her open, trembling as she did.

Elle had no idea what she was doing. She had never used her mouth on a woman like this before; only in her fantasies had she dared. But Kate had already revealed exactly what to do to get her off. Elle silently sent her thanks to the woman before taking a breath and slipping her tongue between Kate's pussy lips.

The taste was unlike anything she'd ever had in her mouth before. It tasted mostly of vinegar and left a thin film on her tongue. She could hear moans bubbling from Kate's mouth, and it spurred her on.

Her tongue wiggled upwards, intent on finding the bundle of nerves that held the key to Kate's orgasm. Alex was huffing behind her, holding back his own climax while his body quaked. His hands were gripping her so tightly that they'd leave bruises. She could feel his shaking through those tense fingers.

It was so much, being stretched so thoroughly while she worked with her tongue. She had never felt anything like the sensations now flooding through every nerve of her body. With a whimper, she sucked and licked with a desperation she didn't know existed within her until now.

It was all moving so quickly. Between the pounding in her ass, and the euphoria of being so *full,* Elle was hard-pressed to hold back. Her orgasm was blooming steadily, taking seed deep in her belly and spreading pulsing roots through her center. The blindfold brought such sweet ignorance, but also the frustration of wanting to watch it happen. Next time, she'd want to see everything.

Kate began grinding her hips into Elle's face. She managed to maintain her pressure on Kate's clit anyway, holding tight with suction and a wriggling tongue to bring Kate closer to climax. She was rewarded as a gush of fluid poured over her face. Elle closed her eyes, relishing in the moment. Kate had told her this might happen.

She had made her *squirt.*

Alex roared as his hips began driving into her erratically. She took that as her cue and allowed herself to tumble over the edge. It was less a fall and more of a fling, because as soon as her orgasm hit, she was flying. Elle threw her head back and cried out as loudly as she ever had. Her throat was raw and dry, and she desperately wanted more beer.

And more sex.

***

Afterward, they fell into a heap on the pillows. Alex stroked Elle's back while Kate removed the blindfold and the cuffs.

"We'll get to use these next time," she said, running a finger down Elle's face.

"We're so happy you decided to join us. This was incredible," Alex said.

Elle smiled wide, showing her teeth, and opened her eyes to see Kate's grin reflecting her own.

"Yeah, me, too. Thank you. I don't think I would have had the courage to do it without you two."

Ever since they had met, the three of them had incredible chemistry. Elle had been a good girl, shy and ignorant of the things that Alex and Kate would often joke about, which had led to her being the odd one out. When Alex and Kate had gotten together, she'd cried for days. It had been confusing for her at the time, because she was mourning the loss of being able to date *either* of them. That had been what had opened her eyes to the fact that she was into women.

When they'd proposed she join them, she had balked at first. But then the thought had taken of her, and she'd fantasized about it constantly. Finally, Elle had confessed that she wanted to go forward with it. Naturally, Kate and Alex were both patient, gentle, and firm in their need for informed consent.

No matter how they'd all found themselves in this room, Elle was grateful. Her ass hurt, and she was sore from the force of her orgasm, but she was bathing in a bliss she'd never known before.

Alex cradled her while Kate gathered snacks and drinks for all of them. After all, they needed to be well-hydrated and fueled for round two.

Three's a Party

Maya isn't sure about her new boy toy... but he's sure about her. When his friends join the mix, things get a little messy and a lot more hot.

There was music playing, an indie tune with a Southern twang. Maya lifted her beer slowly. She scanned the room from over the butt of the bottle, sipping on the scene she could survey from her perch in the corner. It was a packed crowd tonight. There was no sign of–

Oh, no, there he was.

Maya leaned forward, bottle dangling forgotten in her slackened hand. There he was, in all his glory. Shaggy, blonde hair framed his gorgeous face, with deep, brown eyes that made her heart flutter.

They'd been flirting nonstop over text. Maya had kinks she may have spilled to him one night after a few too many martinis. He had responded in kind, divulging some of his own. It had spiraled into conversations that made her stomach flutter every time they replayed in her head.

Daniel found her quickly. He met her gaze, dragged his own down her body, and then slowly back up to her face. Her back tensed, shivers cascading at the base of her spine.

And then, he turned on heel and walked to the bar.

She wasn't sure how to react or what to do next. He hadn't motioned to her, hadn't greeted her. What if their back-and-forth was just something he did with his flavor of the week?

Oh, my God. Am I a fucking flavor of the week? The thought made her shudder for an entirely new set of reasons. Maya wasn't ashamed of sleeping around. However, she also couldn't stand the idea that some man had been able to work his way past her defenses so easily, just to toss her aside in favor of a new toy.

"Hey, you're not like the other girls, huh?"

Maya blinked. She turned her head and wrinkled her nose immediately. A lanky, sweaty man was standing next to her, beer sloshing as he swayed.

"Excuse me?" she asked flatly.

"You're not like these other bitches. I can tell," he yelled over the noise.

"Oh, my God. No," she responded.

"Whaddya mean *no*?" he slurred back.

Instead of responding, Maya popped up from her stool and pushed past him. She was rewarded with a spray of alcohol that soaked the front of her black dress. Naturally, this would happen. She'd finally decided to let her freak flag fly with some hot guy she barely knew, and now that she was about to approach him, she was covered in some drunk dude's backwash.

Fucking awesome.

She was about to pack it in for the night when she glanced over to where Daniel was sitting. He was sprawled on a couch, legs spread wide, elbow on the armrest with his hand holding up his face. She froze in place.

Daniel lazily raised a hand and motioned for her to come to him with two fingers, curling them salaciously. With her cheeks blazing but her feet moving of their own accord, Maya began walking toward the Adonis holding her under his spell. When she approached, he patted his lap, and Maya froze.

"Don't make me put you on my lap, Maya, or you might end up over my knee instead of sitting on it."

Heat blazed through her cheeks, chest, and in that tender place between her legs. She gaped like a fish until he raised an eyebrow, and then she slid down slowly into his lap. Daniel pulled her legs up so that they were resting on the couch and her ass was close to his crotch. He was cradling her with such an ease that they could have easily been mistaken for a couple.

The entire situation was surreal. How she had gone from giving up entirely to sitting in the lap of the man she wasn't even sure she liked was beyond her. Maya glanced over at Daniel, loosely holding her hip with one hand and using the other to gesture as he spoke to a friend. If being his flavor of the week behind closed doors was bad, being so in the public eye was downright catastrophic.

What was she even doing?

Maya wanted to speak up, wanted to say something, anything. She felt frozen, and Daniel made no move to introduce her to any of the people around them. She sat there quietly, frozen in place. She didn't know any of these people; she didn't recognize them from other get-togethers they had been a part of.

"Are you okay?" Daniel asked. He seemed genuinely concerned.

"What? Yeah, fine, I'm fine. Why?" She sputtered out, swallowing hard and avoiding his eyes.

"Your leg has been going nonstop. Also, you're

kind of wet."

Maya pulled a sharp breath through her nose and realized he was right. She had been jiggling her foot, a bad habit of hers that popped up when she was particularly anxious. Daniel was running his hand up and down her back, passively staring as she scrambled to respond.

"I don't know," she finally sighed. "Honestly, I think I'm just confused about this. Also, some guy spilled his drink on me." Maya gestured between them with her pointer finger.

"What's there to be confused about? I thought we were on a date."

Her eyes widened marginally as the concept slammed home. This was a date. They had spent the previous night sexting until the early hours. He'd asked if she wanted to meet up, and she'd agreed.

At the time, she hadn't thought it was a date. She just thought they were…

Oh, no, I'm just stupid, Maya thought glumly. She'd missed the signs, and it had never occurred to her that this god of a man would indulge her further than a digital booty call. Looking back, she felt the flush of shame burn her face. It was a little fucked up to assume the person you wanted was just some shallow hornball.

Maya was interrupted by the back of his fingers brushing against her cheek.

"How about another drink, baby?"

Her lips, stained black to match the rest of her

ensemble, parted. "I'd like that."

"Hey, Mike, can you grab Maya a Bahama Mama?" Daniel called out to somebody across the room. Mike gave him a thumbs-up and headed toward the bar.

"Aren't you going to ask what I drink?" she questioned.

"You said you liked Bahama Mamas last night."

While they spoke, he laid one arm across her lap and held her hip with his hand. The other continued to graze up and down her back. His bedroom eyes seemed to reflect her own darkest desires back to her. They must have been, because that was all she could think about– how he'd taste when he came down her throat, how his cock would slam into every spot that made her see stars.

They sat in silence for a few moments. Maya laid her head down on his shoulder, her nose fitting perfectly against the curve of his neck. His scent was earthy and a little sweet, like the way decaying leaves perfumed the autumn air.

That was her favorite season.

Daniel wrapped his arms around her waist and back, pulling her closer to him. Her heart hammered away when his thumb began brushing against her arm. It was such a comforting gesture, a reminder that he wanted her. She felt the same.

"Hey, here's your drink."

Mike had returned with the promised bright orange-red glass. Maya smiled weakly at him as she took it, briefly wondering whether she should drink it. There was always the chance that this man couldn't be trusted.

Maya pressed the straw between her lips and took a short sip.

"Oh, that's delightful!" she said, smiling at the man who'd made it.

"Thanks! I gotta get back to work, but you kids have fun."

"Yeah, okay, Grandpa," Daniel scoffed, grinning as he said it.

Mike winked and walked off.

Daniel's left hand had moved from her waist to her thigh. The jersey-knit long dress she wore had a slit up to her hip, her leg almost entirely exposed to her upper thigh. Maya felt herself blush once again, realizing she could have been flashing the entire bar and she wouldn't even have known.

"Do you like that?" The husky whisper sent a shiver up her arms and down into her shoulder blades. She practically quivered under the weight of his desire. She was fucked. All the man had said was a single sentence. She couldn't be this hot for him already. It was embarrassing.

"Uhm, yeah," she whispered back, her voice shaking as he nuzzled her neck. Maya wasn't necessarily uncomfortable with public displays of affection, but it was unusual for her to be sat in the lap of some mystery man she'd only recently met.

Whether it was right or wrong, she was deeply enjoying his affection. Maya was finally settling into the idea that perhaps this one could be good. There was something about how tenderly he touched her that made her stomach flutter. She felt silly for second-guessing his intentions earlier.

The ruckus all around them disappeared, and she was swept up by the moment. Time seemed to stand still.

Maya turned her head, lips centimeters from his, and she spoke softly.

"Do you wanna taste my drink?"

"Absolutely, yeah."

She closed the distance, turning her head before their noses could bump. Their lips touched only barely at first, but soon they were locked in a passionate kiss.

"Let's go outside." Daniel pulled back, breathing heavier. "Finish your drink first. We're not allowed to take them with us, and I don't trust them sitting here alone."

That was enough justification for her. It didn't feel like he was just trying to get her drunk. Besides, she could stop if she felt uncomfortable. She was a thirty-year-old woman and no longer as impressionable as she had been in her youth.

Then again, at thirty, she should know how to behave herself in public. Instead, she was acting like a horny teenager. Maya blanched at the thought, catching Daniel's eye again.

"You've got a lot going on up here, huh?" he said, gently tapping her temple with a finger.

"I guess," she laughed, "but that's a helluva way to put it."

"We're going to work on that," he whispered, eyes glistening as he leaned forward once more. "When you're with me, I don't want you to think about anything except for us."

There it was. He had promised her that he had a Dominant side, and she'd told him she'd love to test his patience. It had been a riskier portion of their banter the previous night, and Maya knew that she was playing with fire. She was fine with being burned.

She swallowed, her throat suddenly dry, and brought the straw back to her lips. The drink went down like juice. She finished it in under a minute.

And then the brain freeze hit.

"Oh, ow!" Maya spat out, pressing a hand to her forehead.

"What's wrong?" His tone was urgent, perhaps more so than the situation called for. She studied his furrowed brow for a moment, noting the deep lines that were tight around the intensity of his eyes.

"Just brain freeze," she squeaked. Her eyes squeezed shut. His arms, still tight around her, began to shake. She realized he was laughing.

"Oh, my God. This is so not funny!"

"It's a little funny."

"Fuck off."

They spoke between bouts of giggles, his embrace making her feel warm and secure. Maya was smiling widely, revealing her gleaming teeth.

"Damn, those sure are some canines," Daniel

said, cupping her cheek and running a thumb over their points.

"Oh, yeah. People call them my vampire teeth." She playfully hissed, face now twisting with a wry smile that curled her lips and wrinkled her nose.

"All the better to bite me with."

There was something so deliciously dark about the way he said it, as though he was threatening her. She liked it.

"Planning on doing anything that'll make me want to bite you?"

"Depends. Are you planning on behaving yourself?"

She leaned forward, whispered, "Never," and she stood up. The bar had started to clear out, about half the people remaining. They made their way to the door hand in hand. Her black heels clacked lightly against the hardwood floor. It was barely noticeable above the murmur of voices lilting around them.

Outside, the sun had sunk deep into the horizon. The sunset threw fiery smears of orange and red across the sky, a stark contrast to the deeply bruised twilight. Maya breathed the night air deep into her lungs. A heavy buzz had made her head feel pleasantly light.

It felt like it was going to be a good night. She did have to pee, though.

"I just want a cigarette, and then we can go in," she said, rummaging around in her little cross-body bag. It was a nasty habit, she knew, but nicotine had a hold on her that she couldn't figure out how to break.

"Fine by me," he said, hands in his back pockets as he rocked back slowly onto his heels.

She wasn't certain where this was heading or if there would be a *them* further down the road. For now, she was content in finding a sense of companionship here. She was finding that she liked Daniel quite a bit.

Once she was done with her cigarette, she crushed it out and stuck the stub back in the pack. Daniel took her hand, and they walked back in. She kind of had to pee, but figured it could wait for a little bit. She didn't want to lose the magic building between them. There was a feverish tingle in her breast, like her heart was throwing sparks every time his eyes met hers.

Maya was just hoping that she set his chest ablaze in the same way he did for her.

They sat back down, and Mike was there almost immediately with another drink.

"Okay, fine, but this is the last one," she laughed.

"I think that's a good idea," Daniel murmured into her neck, nuzzling against her again.

"Mmm." Her response was a low, purring sound of approval.

Back in his lap and sipping lightly at her drink, Maya was entirely comfortable, aside from the growing pressure in her lower stomach.

"A few of my friends are coming to hang out with us. The ones we talked about."

Maya felt her entire diaphragm contract. The

friends he was referring to were in the same community as her and Daniel: BDSM. Since moving to the area, she hadn't been very involved in the kink scene. It was a terrifying prospect to meet new people who shared their lifestyle.

Because the community was so small, making a good impression was paramount. Maya worried that she would do nothing but make a fool out of herself. Her only saving grace was that Daniel was essentially her Dominant now. Basically. At least, that's what she told herself. So it would make sense if she stayed quiet and deferred to him. They had no idea what type of Sub she was.

There were three men, dressed well but casually, along with a woman who had on a bright yellow sundress and a pair of wedge heels that Maya thought were adorable.

"I love your dress!" she said, meeting the woman's kind, blue eyes.

"Oh, gosh, thank you!" When she smiled, the corners of her eyes crinkled.

"Before you two get any further, this is Maya," Daniel cut in, squeezing Maya with the arm he had around her waist. She was pleasantly tipsy—not so much that she felt out of control, but just enough that things were a little brighter and everything seemed that much funnier.

They exchanged greetings, and Maya learned that the light-haired woman was Heather. It felt like a suitable name. She thought of her heather-gray sweater and how cozy she felt snuggled into it. This woman seemed like a hug in human form. The other two were Jay and Austin, less interesting to her but pleasant all the same.

Maybe it was the alcohol talking, but she liked these people already.

After getting Heather's order, Jay and Austin headed over to the bar. The place was clearing out, but there were still enough people for there to be a wait. Maya briefly wondered what time it was and how close they were to closing.

"I kind of have to pee," Maya whispered to Daniel, putting her hand on his forearm to pry it off. Instead of releasing her, he held her tighter.

"Just hold it for a little bit. You can go before we leave."

She was getting uncomfortable, but obeying him felt so natural. Maya squeezed her thighs, tightening her pelvic muscles to hold it together. The friction between her legs shot sharp, little spikes into her pussy. She breathed a little harder, shifting to find a more comfortable position.

Daniel rubbed his finger over her once-again exposed thigh, and Maya stifled a moan. Goosebumps rose to reveal the trail his hands took as he explored the expanse of exposed flesh she was offering.

"You're squirming." His lips were centimeters away from the cuff of her ear, breath drifting out in puffs, pleasantly ticklish and warm. Maya widened her eyes, clenching her thighs even harder. This time, it wasn't inspired by the building pressure in her abdomen. The threat seemed clear to her: sit still and be good, or face the consequences.

Her face brightened even further as she remembered them detailing a few fantasies, filling out these little forms that went over their kinks, their limits, and more. They had exchanged test results and bantered until the early morning hours.

After they'd stopped messaging each other, Maya had crawled under the covers and slipped a bullet vibrator between her legs. It wasn't his looks that got her. Instead, Maya felt helplessly swept up by his gentle nature and sense of humor. She was so glad she hadn't let her lack of self-esteem get the best of her.

She was snapped from her thoughts when she felt soft skin skimming against her exposed thigh. It made her shift again, reminding her of the pressure building in her pelvis, and she shivered with desperation.

"Okay, seriously, I'm gonna head to the bathroom," she giggled, swinging her legs out of his lap and nearly toppling to the floor.

"I think you might need a little help, baby," Daniel laughed as he steadied her, one hand holding hers and the other on her hip. Maya flushed at the idea that she couldn't even go to the bathroom by herself. Perhaps she had overindulged just a little.

Heather smiled and told Daniel she needed to go too, so she would help Maya. Taking her by the hand, Heather led Maya to the bathroom. They giggled wordlessly, huddled together as they walked like careless schoolgirls. On the way, Maya learned that Heather was getting a Ph.D. in Philosophy and looking to move abroad once her doctoral program was over. Maya loved learning about people's lives. It seemed as though everybody she met had a rich, detailed background just waiting to be discovered.

Once they were in the bathroom, Maya was spun against the wall, Heather's body pressed against hers. She made a soft sound when her back made impact, but was silent aside from that. A moment hung between them that Maya was terrified to shatter because of what it could mean.

"Do you like this?" Heather whispered, eyes staring steadily into Maya's. Her hand had come up to cup her face. Maya shuddered and leaned into the warm touch.

"Yes."

With that approval, Heather leaned forward, and their lips met in a feverish rush. She had come here for one Dom, but it looked like she was going to score with another. What a night. She didn't think Daniel would complain, especially if this led somewhere else and he was able to join.

Kissing women was one of the things Maya liked to think she did best. She craved the softness, the silken hair and the smooth skin and the gentle lips.

Well, sometimes gentle. Right now, there was nothing *gentle* about what they were doing.

Heather had a fistful of her hair, teeth scraping

against Maya's bared neck. Their sounds were animalistic. She couldn't help but wonder if it was the instant attraction she felt for this woman or if it was the alcohol, but it was exactly what she needed.

The door opened, and Maya threw Heather away from her on instinct.

It was Daniel.

"Daniel?" she slurred, brows furrowing.

"You were taking a while, so I came to see what was going on. That's really fucking nice of both of you, honestly."

"Oh, God, Daniel, I'm so sorry–"

"Shut up, Maya, and bend over the sink."

"I just– What?" She stopped short.

"You heard me."

Maya was to her left, Daniel in front of her. The sink, just behind.

"You heard me. How naughty of you. I would have thought you'd know better."

She realized that he was dead serious when he started unbuckling his belt. Her knees were weak.

"Be a good girl, Maya," Heather said in a voice far more sultry than before. Her blue eyes were frigid with a malice that gave Maya pause.

Slow as she dared, Maya turned and took the steps necessary to arrive at the sink. Daniel slid his belt through its loops, slowly doubling it in his hands and snapping the leather against itself. She winced, her heart skipping a beat at the booming crack.

"Do you know why you're being punished?"

"I–" Her voice cracked, so she cleared her throat. "I made out with Heather without your permission."

"No."

Maya's eyes shot to his in the mirror, confusion blooming on her face.

"You're being punished because you acted like a little slut at the first opportunity."

She didn't have enough time to rebut before he stepped forward, pulled his arm back, and spanked her across the ass with his belt. Her vision nearly went black as pain screamed through every nerve in her exposed ass. Perhaps she had gone a little far in her confessions when sleep deprivation had loosened her tongue. This was moving so fast, it felt like her head would spin right off of her shoulders.

Maya was gripping the sink so hard that her knuckles had turned white at the center, fading into red. Her eyes were locked on Daniel's in the mirror. She watched as he smiled, a sinister thing, and offered Heather the belt. She took it from him and positioned herself behind Maya.

"And one from me for good measure," she said, bringing her arm back and swinging. Maya yelped again, her entire body tensing and lunging forward from the fierce sting. It left her feeling warm and woozy, even as her soaked panties betrayed her arousal. Impact play, with two Dominants? How could she be so lucky?

"Come here."

Daniel was now sitting on the chair across from the sink. His legs were spread lazily, shaggy hair falling over his intense eyes. His button-down shirt had opened, revealing a t-shirt that looked buttery soft. Maya wanted to push her face into his barrel chest and get lost in his scent.

She did as she was told, choosing to fall to her knees in front of him. If it pleased him, she would worship at his altar all night long. And, of course, there was still Heather. Maya dared a look over her shoulder to see her watching with hawk-sharp eyes.

"Take my cock out, Maya."

Maya could feel steam rising from her skin as she reached for him.

Her hands shook as she undid the button on his jeans, pulling them open to reveal briefs and the straining manhood tenting them. Maya pulled the boxers down a little so that his cock was on proud display. She nearly choked. It was the largest she had ever seen outside of porn. Wherever it was going, she wasn't sure it was going to fit.

"Use your mouth, baby. Show me how sorry you are for being a little whore," Daniel said, his voice low and gravely. Maya scrambled to obey, placing her mouth over his tip, hovering for a moment before she took him into her mouth and began bobbing up and down.

He was already salty with pre-cum. Briefly, she wondered what had done it. Was it her tight ass rubbing against his cock while she sat in his lap? Was it the thought of her and Heather, lip-locked and tongues swirling? Or maybe he had started leaking his arousal when he had spanked her ass.

These thoughts and more ran through her mind as she gagged and choked on him. Her hands reached out, taking the thick shaft in a soft grip, and she began twisting them in opposite directions. Daniel let loose a low groan of approval, his head falling back in abject ecstasy.

She felt Heather slip up behind her, stomach pressed into Maya's back. Her hands came around to play with her tits through her bra, and Maya whimpered as she continued to serve Daniel as best she could.

"What a good girl you are," Heather crooned into her ear, "sucking that cock so good. But I think we can go deeper, can't we?"

Maya felt a hand wrap around the back of her neck, pushing down and encouraging her to take Daniel's cock deeper. She was gagging now and desperate for air. It was almost over, though. She could feel his hips thrusting up into her mouth, pushing himself into her throat.

Her mouth filled with his hot, thick cum in jetting spurts as he found his release. Maya groaned, Heather whispering into her ear, "Swallow it, slut."

It went down harshly. Maya had never been a fan of cum in her mouth, but with Heather demanding to see it? Oh, she would swallow every day of the week to please this domineering Domme. She hadn't expected any of this out of the petite blonde, but she was so happy to be so thoroughly surprised.

Maya rested her head on Daniel's thigh, gasping for breath.

"I hope you aren't tired, baby girl, because I want my turn."

Maya felt her belly flutter. Heather's words reignited something inside of her. Regardless of how tired she was now, she would keep going just to hear that sexy, raspy voice issuing humiliating commands.

This was everything.

"Yes, ma'am," she whispered in response.

Under Pressure

Imogen has one thing on her mind... and for once, it isn't work. With the pressure building externally *and* internally, can she keep quiet?

PAIRING:

MF

KINKS INCLUDED:

Piss Play, Impact Play,
Shower Sex, Drunk Sex

SPICE LEVEL:

3/10

CHARACTERS:

Ethan, Imogen

Steam billowed in swirling pillars, glowing yellow in the soft candlelight. Flaring heat set her lower belly alight with a radiance to rival the flitting flames scattered throughout the bathroom.

It was almost time.

The sound of water drumming against the shower floor became a steady rhythm that soothed her fraying nerves. Soon, the warm pebbles of water raining down would become her downfall.

They always did this in the dark. At first, fucking by candlelight in the shower felt odd. It was spooky how their tangled bodies cast strange shadows across the white walls and floors. The shapes coalesced into a writhing mass with flailing limbs, a strange monster that she caught out of the corner of her eye. A few times, she had jumped, thinking it was a person. The idea made her pussy throb. The threat of hidden, leering eyes never failed to whet her appetite. Monster or man, she would gladly take whatever savage cock waited for her.

Imogen's clit was pinched between the unrelenting teeth of a clothespin, nipples in the same predicament. She gritted her teeth against the sharp throb that drove her to madness every time she was in trouble. Jared was a sadist to his core, and he loved watching her suffer on her knees beneath him. He had even applied heating gel before he'd placed his chosen instruments, all the while whispering about what he was going to do to her next.

Sex toys were laid out next to her, along with a full bottle of wine. It struck her as funny that the illustrated label should lean so medieval when he was about to subject her to torture straight from the Dark Ages. Imogen kept her eyes downcast and her hands folded, aiming to appease as much as she could.

Ethan returned just as the pressure became nearly unbearable. She was surrounded by a thick shroud of mist, settling around her as it accumulated. It clouded the room in those sliding shadows that sent shuddering shivers down her spine.

Imogen bit her lip and waited for his next command. She didn't receive them often. She was an executive at her company. All day long, she directed and commanded other people. On nights like these, there was nothing but resolute obedience to a man who had proved himself to be worthy of her submission.

She watched as his shins came closer, then disappeared as he dipped down. He kneeled in front of her, still tall enough to tower even when he brought himself down to her level. Ethan used a finger to lift her chin. She kept her eyes downcast even still.

"Look at me."

The command was quiet, nearly impossible to hear over the soft roar of the shower. Imogen did as she was bidden, rolling her green eyes slowly up until she was gazing at him through her thick lashes. Ethan was still wearing the suit that he hated. Ever the artist, he spent most days in a smock, surrounded by pottery to glaze and canvases to paint.

Today, he'd attended a black tie event that had

demanded his best. It had likely been at some point during a simpering encounter with a potential buyer that Ethan had decided her fate for the night. It was power he could readily wield when everything else felt out of his hands.

Her tawny skin was moist. Speckled droplets rose along her skin, gathering like morning dew. When Ethan placed a finger at the bottom of her slit and dragged it upwards across her keening cunt, it was a different moisture he was collecting. He pinched her cheeks between his thumb and pointer finger in one, pressing the glistening finger to her lips with the other.

Imogen opened her mouth and heard him draw a breath through his clenched teeth. She sucked faithfully, removing every trace of herself from his skin, until he told her it was enough. Releasing her face, now red from the vice-like grip, Ethan moved his hand between her legs once more. This time, it was to remove the horrible clothespin still clinging to her swollen, reddened clit. Mercifully, he took it off, and then the two clinging to either nipple.

Despite herself, she whimpered as he tugged the handle, a vicious smile creeping across his lips.

"Such a little slut for pain," he crooned, voice sickly sweet as he praised her, "My bad girl just can't keep her mouth shut, can she?"

She shuddered in anticipation. She had displeased him. He had told her that he required her silence, since she'd been so naughty lately. Tonight was a lesson in self-discipline. It had only just begun, and Imogen was already failing the test miserably.

"Fetch me a toy and get your drink. Crawl," he whispered, almost unheard over the spray of the shower.

The sound liquified her spine.

He had brought a tub of ice cubes with him. Fear and desire mingled, leaking into one another as her heart fell but her lower belly floated. Imogen began the short crawl to her dreaded destination. Her heart hammered hard enough to bend metal, striking the copycat pulse between her legs like it was an anvil.

Imogen managed to clutch the neck of the bottle between one set of fingers and a small, red bullet vibrator in her palm. Pain erupted as she felt a flat hand strike her ass, and she let loose a sound between a breathless moan and a sharp yelp. A horrible silence followed. She had managed to hold onto both objects, which gave her a faint glimmer of hope. Crawling back to him, she placed the bottle and vibrator at his feet, kneeling with her hands flat on either thigh. Her nipples hurt.

"Are you satisfied, slut?" he ground out, "Come here. Turn around and lie between my legs."

Her pussy quivered as she gingerly twisted, pushing herself toward him until she was seated with her back against his chest. Imogen could feel his hard cock pressing into the small of her back. He leaned forward, wrapping an arm around her waist, and snatched up the bottle. It had already been uncorked, a decorative stopper protecting the contents instead.

Ethan popped it out of the top, handing her the

bottle.

"Drink."

Imogen took a long, gulping drag from the bottle. The thick wine coated her tongue in a delightful tang.

"I'm going to play with your pretty pussy until you're done with the bottle. You don't get to cum until it's all gone."

Imogen wanted to whimper, to push her face into his neck and beg for his lenience. Even if she did, he would not give it to her. There was only cruelty in this place of darkness he led her to when they both needed to let go. She'd developed not just a taste for pain here but a deep hunger that gnawed ceaselessly. A beast had been born that could be gentled only through violence.

He spread her wet pussy with two fingers, the other hand holding the vibrator. With a long press of his thumb, the toy came to life. The setting was low, but that wouldn't matter. It might as well have been pumped to the highest level with all the other points of pleasure he had to toy with, plump and sensitive from the clothespins.

The impact with that engorged bundle of nerves was jarring. Electric pleasure ripped through her torso, and her grip tightened on the bottle until her fingers turned white, then slowly red.

Imogen's hands shook as she brought the wine to her mouth, tipping it back to drink deeply. She squeezed her eyes shut and tried to keep her hips still while he did his best to break her. Moving away from him would only end in a harsh punishment. She needed to control herself.

The next gulp nearly choked her, but it meant that half the bottle was gone. Her head began to swim with intoxication. It served only to stoke the fire Ethan was carefully tending. As she pulled the glass from her lips to breathe, Imogen realized there was a new pressure entering the gray—her bladder was filling.

As soon as she realized it, the thumping pleasure arrived. It tingled at first, the sensation arousing, but it built to a feverish intensity at the need to relieve herself. It was a torturous sort of delight that shredded any semblance of self-respect left; her ego entirely dissolved, dissipating as the delicious, forbidden feelings bloomed between her legs. It had taken months to admit her kink to him. She'd been shocked at how quickly he'd moved to indulge her as soon as he'd found out.

Imogen winced when his other hand lifted to her face, once again pinching her so hard that she could feel her cheeks push through her teeth. Her mouth opened, and she panted as he began whispering dirty, terrible things into her ear.

"You're so pretty when you're so desperate." He paused to roll her earlobe between his teeth, "Does it hurt yet, Imogen? I bet the pressure is unbearable between those pretty legs." She could only jerk stiffly in his arms, face contorting as wave after wave of need for release crashed into the weeping shore of her dripping center. Tears threatened to spill over her cherry-red cheeks.

It was too much.

"You did this to yourself," he hissed, grinding the

vibrator into her clit until she finally let out a frantic yelp.

Everything stopped. Imogen tried to catch her breath, still painfully full in her lower belly, while Ethan guided her up from his lap. He stood up and looked down at her.

"Take an ice cube and put it in that tight pussy. Stay on your knees, and keep those knees under your hips. For every ice cube you drop, I'll spank you once."

Her heart nearly stopped. It was an almost impossible task, but there was a chance her clenched muscles would be able to keep an ice cube in place, even as it burned against the heat of her slick walls.

Imogen reached a hand into the bucket and picked a cube—a large one—out of the pile. She could hear the pounding, erratic thump of her heart as she did as she was told and slipped the ice inside of herself. At first, it was almost a pleasant sensation, cooling her heated body. As soon as she adjusted to holding onto it, the burn began.

She could have wept from the sensations warring for dominance inside of her. Her bladder was putting pressure on the clitoral systems that ran deep into the pelvic area. Her contracted muscles bore down on the sensitive nerves. If she held it long enough, she always came from that alone. Ethan could force her to come just by pouring drinks down her throat and holding her down, watching her writhe as she fought against the humiliating act of pissing herself.

Imogen got off purely from her physiology.

Ethan got off purely from watching her suffer.

She loved the calloused pervert in him deeply. This version of him, so different from the protective, gentle man she married, thrilled and captivated her. Imogen winced as the ice started melting. Long trails of dripping water descended down her leg, a mixture of arousal and evidence of the shrinking cube.

Still, she held on.

He was taking his time putting the toys away. It was likely that he'd taken out far more than they'd need so he could make her wait longer, thighs crushed together, close to overflowing in so many ways. Once finished, Ethan approached her, gripping her chin. He jerked her face up to look into his.

She kept her eyes downcast.

"Imogen, look at me."

His husky voice added another rich layer to the full-body experience gripping her tight. Imogen slowly met his gaze, tears once again beading at the corners of her watering eyes.

"I'm impressed. You were a very good girl for me. Keep it up and I'll let you come. If not, it's going to be a very long, restless night for you."

She remained silent as he released her face and led her into the steaming shower. They had overhead showerheads that rained hot, soothing water like a thick sheet of rain. The instant the heat hit her body, Imogen felt herself separate; it seemed as though her mind was leaving her body. Ethan's strong arms reached over and held her.

"Be careful," he murmured into her ear. "If you hurt yourself, you'll have an incredibly sore bottom once you've recovered."

Imogen nearly moaned in response. The idea of his strong hand landing square on her ass, her wiggling hips desperate to escape the pain while she helplessly cried out… It was enough to almost break her. Almost.

He had a small, waterproof vibrator in his hand. She bit her lip and sucked in a breath through her nose. Her hair was slick and straight, soaked through now beneath the cascade.

"Imogen." He pressed his forehead to hers, "Get on your knees and be a good girl for me."

The rivulets of water were thicker now, warm on her jaw and lips. She sank down, kneeling tall. He handed her the vibrator wordlessly. She took it hesitantly, turned it on, and gave him what he wanted.

Imogen spread her pussy wide and ground the vibrator hard into that tender bundle of nerves that both begged to be sated and pleaded to be left untouched. Her cries echoed off the walls into a cacophony of horrible, unbearable pleasure.

She was so full. So, *so* deliciously full. Imogen was weeping now. Ethan crouched behind her, bringing his hands around to play with her tender nipples while she screamed and cried. His lips began trailing tender kisses down her nape, a line of firecracker pops that made her shudder and shake.

"Please…" She finally broke, her voice ringing out

shrill and on the brink of breaking.

"Please what, princess? Use your words," he growled into her ear, pulling her head back with his hand, biting into her neck.

"I need… I just want… Please, it hurts, I need to…" Her words came in a stuttering, halting rhythm. She could hardly hold it any longer.

With one last primal call, she released the flood that had put so much pressure on every point of pleasure hidden deep beneath her skin. Her urine flooded the shower floor as her body convulsed. Not once did she remove the vibrator from her clit, relishing in the sharp pain that zapped in short bursts through her torso when her climax faded and another began building.

Finally, it was over. Imogen felt faint from the steam, combined with the effort of holding herself together for so long. It came crashing down and she curled into Ethan, sighing gently against his chest. It was something close to sleeping, but not quite there. He washed them both, cradling her languorous body.

Eventually, Imogen drifted off.

***

When she woke, it was to the sensation of Ethan picking her up bridal-style. He carried her into their bedroom, a much smaller room than she could have liked. They'd had to sacrifice for the bathroom, and that *was* her favorite room.

It was, after all, where the shower was.

Ethan laid her carefully on the bed, tracing a gentle line down her cheek with his thumb when she looked up at him.

"You did so good for me, princess. You behaved yourself so well."

"I spoke out of turn."

"Mmm. You did. But we'll deal with that later. For now, you need to sleep."

"I love you."

"I love you, too."

She felt her eyes falling closed, imagery of the punishments he would impose filling her head as she fell asleep.

DARKNESS & SPICE

Knot Without a Fight

Simon and Sierra are two shifters with one problem between them: Sierra's painful heats. Luckily, Simon knows just how to cure her.

PAIRING:

MF

KINKS INCLUDED:

Breeding, Knotting, Fluff,
CNC, Primal Play

SPICE LEVEL:

4/10

CHARACTERS:

Simon, Sierra

SIERRA

Everything smelled sharper around this time of the month. The sour, salty scent of her husband's sweat was hot on her tongue, as he split logs a few feet away. Warmth from her cocoa cup seeped into her chilled hands, a welcome protection against the cool autumn air.

Simon always knew how to take care of her.

The weather had a frosted edge, and it made her bones ache. Sierra was restless as it was, the lunar swelling triggering a chain of reactions inside her body. The call of the wild was impossible to resist. That was why she was here, in a cabin hours away from town.

She and Simon had saved up to afford a down payment on a cottage where they could stay during her heat. It was a place where flowers grew in thick swaths across rolling hills, framed by a forest pregnant with plentiful prey to hunt. The moss was soft beneath her feet, and the balcony of branches above let through just enough moonlight to cast a silvery sheen across everything

At the sound of a whistle, Sierra glanced up. Her husband was outfitted in true lumberjack fashion, and she'd teased him for it earlier. His red flannel was rolled at the sleeves, with blue jeans and steel-toed boots to match. If the others were there, they'd never let him live it down. She could hear the Paul Bunyan jokes already.

They seldom strayed from the safety and comfort of their pack. This heat called for something different, however. She needed Simon and *only* Simon this time.

There was a voice gnawing at the back of her mind, something obsessive and possessive that demanded his undivided attention. While it was wonderful to fall into a mass of heaving bodies–truly, it was bliss beyond belief– she also craved the sole companionship of the wolf she had married.

Having finally caught her attention, Simon smiled. His bright, straight teeth gleamed in comparison to his deep umber skin. With his green eyes that were framed by thick, black lashes, he had caught her eye immediately, and she hadn't been able to shake that hold since.

He nodded his head toward the house and started back that way, expecting Sierra to follow, so confident in it that he didn't so much as turn around to confirm. But there was no need, because she popped out of the plastic lawn chair and followed him, feet crackling through freshly fallen leaves gathering in their yard.

Her mug sat on the table beside the chair, forgotten.

SIMON

He could hear Sierra coming in behind him, those tiny footsteps sounding off like thunder when the scent of her need wafted to him. It wasn't yet the peak of her heat, but her desire was swelling with the approach of twilight. It was almost impossible to ignore; the ghost of her unique tang lingered in his mouth, summoned by the swollen, dripping cunt between her legs. It was a tease. She was *teasing* him.

Even the distance between them couldn't overcome the strength of her arousal. In an effort to control himself, Simon gritted his teeth, fists forming, nails digging painfully into his palms.

It was a losing battle, but the war would wage all night, and he needed to pace himself. She needed to eat and get ready. There was a dance to this that he needed to respect.

After all, this time, he got her all to himself. When the entire pack came together, it was five hungry wolves chasing Sierra down. They couldn't all be first to the prize. While Simon enjoyed a good game between packmates, he relished in the idea that tonight, he didn't have to compete.

Simon had already prepped dinner and readied dessert. He took care of her in every aspect when her time came. It was not only his duty but his pleasure. There was something so deeply protective in him that yearned for something small to take care of. For now, he would focus that attention on pampering the love of his life.

The thick venison stew filled the kitchen with an aroma that offset what haunted his hungry tongue. A slab of pure Irish butter had been laid on a plate to soften next to the bread he'd baked earlier. Everything was perfect.

When Sierra finally joined him, her scent hit Simon like a freight train. The explosion of desire blew away all rational thought in his brain. He wanted nothing more than to tackle her to the ground and take her. He wanted to fill her with his cock, his seed; he wanted to *breed his bitch.*

Instead, he sniffed heavily and turned toward the stove, trying to hide his rising manhood. If Sierra noticed, she said nothing. It was her way of conveying disinterest. While the nearness of the peak made her desperately horny, it also made her uncomfortable. She was in pain.

Her distress brought him endless agony. It would be a kindness to pin her to the floor and take her when he finally snapped. She'd fight him tooth and claw, but in the war of strength, he always won.

She'd end the night filled with his knot and begging for more. Simon would make sure of it.

In the meantime, he would comfort her as best he could as she grew more and more restless. Food was a good first step. She would need to be fully fueled to endure what the night held in store. His cock began throbbing as he considered what he would do… how he would rip her apart.

Simon jumped when she slid an arm around his stomach from behind.

"What are you doing, sweetness?" he said with a chuckle.

"I just wanted to say I love you," she responded, her head pressed into his broad back.

He stood there, basking in the feel-good hormones flooding his system. His background as a nurse made him all too aware of the physiological elements of their lupine nature.

Sierra slipped away and started toward the slow cooker.

"This smells so good, baby," she threw over her shoulder with a smile. His heart fluttered.

"Well, I hope so. I'd be disappointed if it wasn't," Simon said, walking up behind her. It was his turn to wrap his arms around her. He buried his face in her hair, and she giggled.

"I'd never tell you that your food is bad. You know that."

"Even if it tasted like soggy sneakers?"

"Not even then, darling. Your feelings are too precious to me."

"Thank you for considering my delicate sensibilities."

It ended in a fit of laughter. Even after four years of marriage, they were happy so long as they were together.

SIERRA

She ran her manicured nails through his coarse hair, enjoying the rich texture. He kept it short, but Simon also had the face to pull off any style. *Almost.*

She wouldn't want to see him in a mohawk. Not because it would ruin his looks, but because it would be incredibly silly.

Her blood was running hot. It was thick and slow

in her veins. She could feel every shuddering beat of her heart as it pumped hard in her chest. There was an echo of that rhythm, a persistent pulse between her legs. But there was also discomfort. It wasn't pain yet, exactly, but it was irritating enough to be distracting.

Sierra was particularly sensitive during her heat. Every single brush of clothing against her core reminded her of the desperate conundrum: she *needed* to be touched, but she *wanted* to be sequestered away.

When she'd seen Simon, she had known immediately that he was the one. A *fated mate*, according to some in their community. But it was the way he treated her during her heat and his intuitive nature in figuring out exactly what she needed that had sealed the deal.

She accepted a steaming bowl of stew from him, and they both walked to the little island arm separating the kitchen from the living room. Quietly, Sierra seated herself, tucking into the mouthwatering meal Simon had worked so hard on. The venison was tender enough to tear apart with a fork, and the vegetables retained their form with a little bit of crunch.

He had outdone himself.

Sierra reached for a crusty end of bread. She buttered it lightly before dipping it into the strew and taking a little bite. While she knew she needed to eat, her appetite always took a hit in her condition. But Simon would be upset if she didn't give her body what it needed…

And naughty girls faced consequences for their

actions.

Her cheeks flushed at the thought, and her pussy answered with a desperate shiver that felt like needles. She could feel Simon tense beside her, his spoon halfway to his face. It was her arousal. The sweet, sour scent saturated the air, and she knew he was using all the control he had not to take her then and there.

There would be plenty of time for it later. They had a script they followed faithfully every heat, and it worked perfectly. As hot and bothered as he was, Sierra was confident that he wouldn't break. He never did. For her, he could always hold himself together. The rest of the pack was the same way. No matter how badly they wanted to hunt her, they held themselves back until it was time.

She loved that he was a perfect gentleman—until it came time to bring her to heel and fill her with his cum.

SIMON

Her sweet cunt was calling to him. The desire was a feral animal shrieking in his chest. It chewed desperately at the bars until he worried that his ribs would crack under those fearsome teeth.

Soon, he thought to himself, glancing at the clock. It was nearly time. He could wait a little bit longer.

They finished the meal in tense silence. Simon spent his time imagining every way he was going to fuck her—once he caught her, of course.

Sierra stood up abruptly. Her spoon clanked

against the bowl as she gathered up her dishes to put in the sink. Simon followed right after her, abandoning his half-eaten meal in favor of what they had really come here for. He watched as she slipped away toward the bedroom. Once, she had tried to hide from him in there. He had shown her thoroughly why that was a very bad idea, although it had involved buying a new door.

She still held that one over his head.

No, instead of hiding from him, she'd be disrobing. They had come to an agreement–if she could escape him, he wouldn't touch her. If not, he could do whatever he pleased. There was something inherently erotic about the chase, and even more so about the way he'd cover her and force her to take his throbbing cock.

His manhood twitched at the thought.

Simon gave her fifteen minutes. That was plenty of time to take her clothing off and get a good head start. He loved giving her the false hope of success, that growing light in her eyes when she thought she was close to her first victory. Pride always came before the fall.

The boots in the hallway sat next to a backpack stuffed full of everything he'd need to ensure her best behavior once she was in hand. They were a few of her favorite toys, along with some rope and other odds and ends. Of course, he also included a variety of snacks and some electrolyte-rich drinks for after.

With a racing heart and shaking hands, he readied for the hunt.

SIERRA

Sierra was shaking. Sweat dripped down her face, and her heart was fretful as a frightened rabbit. Her heat was coming into full bloom, and she was in agony. It was a strange sensation–she knew she needed to be fucked hard, but the idea of being touched and knotted by Simon made her stomach flip.

There was also a primal desire to force him to *earn* his mating rights. In the animal kingdom, almost every male had to prove their worth to the females through feats of strength or adoration. Why shouldn't Simon, too, have to prove that he was worthy to mount her?

Her cunt was radiating with shooting pains that felt like lightning licking up her torso. Sierra realized she was panting, and she began ripping her clothing off. She didn't want a single article of clothing touching her. She didn't want *anything* touching her.

She needed a release. It would come in the form of wet, cool grass whipping around her ankles and shins as she raced through their yard into the treeline. The leaves would crackle, brightly crisp underfoot, and the sensation would delight her. This was what she was made for. Wolves were meant to run free. They took blockers to keep the transformation at bay, but the heat and the animalistic behavior remained. It was impossible to fully break a connection so ancient.

Sierra took a shaky breath, carefully padding to the door leading to the back deck. She loved that the bedroom connected to it; this had been a selling point for her. Sliding the glass entrance open and slipping through it, Sierra walked out into a night cold enough to make her shiver. The sun set quickly this time of year.

She took a deep breath, more confidently than before, and then she shot out of the doorway and into the open air.

For a few blessed moments, she forgot it all. Her heat, the hunt, the pain—everything was gone. Sierra's senses were supercharged under the power of Mother Moon, whose pregnant belly called to action the females of their species. The air tasted of sweet, earthy decay, the approach of snow, and prey animals sheltering in place at the threat of her approach. She was, after all, an apex predator. *The* apex predator.

A low growl rumbled from her throat as she slowed to a walk at the tree line. She knew her eyes would be glowing golden at this point. Even the blockers couldn't blot out every part of her nature.

Her body twitched. This was it.

She dove into the forest.

SIMON

He was watching her from the front door, stealing glances from behind the satin curtain that covered the glas. Simon was openly growling and whining now, pacing after she disappeared into the forest.

The minutes left were grinding his nerves to

nothing. Soon, he'd sink his teeth into her soft skin and mark once again what was always his. It never failed to make his cock hard, her insistence that he should fight for the right to fuck her. If Simon was honest, he'd admit that he was a sexual sadist. He loved watching her writhe beneath him, helpless and desperate as she attempted to stave off his advances.

The timer went off, and Simon snapped to attention.

It was finally time.

He threw open the door and ran headlong into the front yard. Sierra's unique tang was still lingering in the sweet, crisp air. Even with the tempting sights and sounds all around, the wolf inside stayed trained on the sickly sweet scent perfuming the air. He wanted his mate, and he wanted her *right fucking now.*

She was his and his alone, and he would prove that to her with nothing but his teeth and cock… and maybe a few toys, too, if she was a good girl for him.

His surroundings had become a tangle of shadows, but Simon's night vision kicked in. It was a powerful asset when weaving through the trees at a breakneck pace in pursuit of his pleasure. Even so, branches scraped at his skin while he sprinted toward her. His desire for her was molten in his pumping veins. Nothing would stand between him and that sweet, dripping pussy taunting him not more than half a mile away.

SIERRA

She could feel him nearby. There was a primitive connection that tied them as thoroughly as his knot after they made love. It was as though his wolfish eyes were watching, leering, just behind her. Sierra shivered.

The pressure between her legs had become nearly unbearable. She was so incredibly *tender*. The pulse there was either quicker than her heartbeat, or her heart was *racing.*

The animal inside, frothing at the mouth, spurred her to run as fast and far as she could away from the panacea of her pain. She knew that Simon's thick, hard cock would extinguish what was burning hot at the apex of her thighs. But knowing and *feeling* were two very different things.

As the moon rose to her zenith, logic broke down further and further until she was made of the wilderness. With rivers for veins, and a weeping willow mane, she would accept every transformation offered by the mother of all things. It was her birthright to do so.

Sierra ran at an impossible speed now, hurtling through the underbrush that tore at her feet, and through mud that squished between her toes and stuck to her soles. Her flowing, dark hair lashed around wildly, at times stinging her eyes when little wisps whipped into her face.

This was joy, pure and undiluted by the weight of her humanity. It was an expulsion of everything that weighed so heavily during the rest of the month. The promise of relief was sometimes the only thing that kept her going. No matter what happened, there would always be this.

Coming to a break in the trees, Sierra skittered to a halt. She was at the edge of a cliff, overlooking a view that made her heart race. Stark naked and covered in mud, she felt as connected to the earth as she ever had. There was something like pride unfolding in her chest; it began as a speck and built to something inconceivable.

A river cut through the landscape. It snaked along through the sea of trees, black and blue in the pale light. There was nothing but the splendor of nature as far as the eye could see. Sierra breathed deep, eyes closed, savoring every intoxicating scent. She didn't notice his approach until a hand clapped over her mouth and she was falling backward.

SIMON

He stood completely still as he watched her. Milky moonlight shone through a patchwork of dark clouds, casting traveling shadows over her naked body. The swell of her hips was cupped by spotlights, as though they called for his hands to reach out and take her.

He could.

He could grab those thick hips and ram his cock deep inside of her tender, swollen cunt. Nothing was stopping him now. Even as she sought to evade him, her nature took over and she made herself easy prey. She needed him to fill her with his cum and mark her as his.

Simon had shed his clothing when she'd paused. It was the perfect time to make his move. She needed a release that only he could bring her. Even in this rapture, he knew her body quivered with aching need.

I'll fix it, baby, he thought. It was time. He wouldn't let her continue to suffer, not when he could take it all away.

Beyond that, his cock was so hard that it hurt.

Simon crept forward, crouching. It was easy. Far too easy, even if she *was* waiting for him. She needed to be more careful. Even if these woods were generally safe, there was always a chance, under the pull of the moon, that another would be hunting in these same shadows. He didn't want to have to kill. He had dedicated his life to others in the nursing field.

But to defend Sierra? He would kill. Ruthlessly. *Viciously*. Without pause or hesitation. There weren't many guarantees in life, but that was one of them.

Once Simon could feel the heat rolling off her body in the frosty stillness, he reached and clamped a hand around her mouth, yanking her backward. After a brief, shocked pause, he was met with resistance, flailing hands and muffled cries.

"Calm down," he snarled, now in a crouch with her against his chest, and he flipped them over so he was pressed against her back. He released her mouth to secure both her hands. Sierra gasped for air, nearly barking with the effort. He felt a twinge in his chest and paused for a moment. It was long enough for her to break her hands free of his grip and twist around, now chest-to-chest with him.

Of course she would prostrate to him, still begging for release while she fought his advances. Even as she grabbed for his throat, her hips bucked into his cock. Simon gasped at the feeling, coughing as her hands circled tighter.

Sierra's nails were digging into his skin now. He could feel the little, red crescents forming, could feel the blood welling from them. Simon growled as pain-laced pleasure shot through him. He had landed square between her legs, and he could feel her slick slit teasing him as they struggled.

"Enough," he finally roared, pulling his hips back, and even while she cried out for mercy, he slammed himself inside of her.

SIERRA

The pain was nearly unbearable. She could feel it radiating through her body with every movement, and there was a *lot* of movement. Oh, how it ached, how her blood called out for his touch. She was desperate for him to fill her with his cum, to breed her under the full moon's call. But she couldn't give it to him. No, net yet.

Not without a fight.

Sierra bucked her hips, knowing the reaction it would get, and she broke free of his grip once he was distracted. If there was one thing she would never forget, no matter how much the beast inside took over, it was that men were stupid.

She grabbed for his neck, panting for breath under the weight of his body. If she could choke him out, she could run and outpace the pain. Her body yearned for the freedom of moving feet and open air.

Instead, Simon shifted, shattered the silence, and then slammed deep inside of her.

If he broke the silence, Sierra obliterated it. The roar that ripped from her throat was nothing short of animalistic, a desperate screech of both impossible pleasure and inconceivable pain. Once the last, whispering trace of her rabid vocalization dissipated, there was nothing but a croaking moan that hitched and cracked.

Simon was gently moving his hips now, as much as she wanted him to fuck her as hard and fast as possible. She could hear his efforts to stay gentle as he took deep, shuddering breaths through clenched teeth.

It was a frantic sort of pleasure. Sierra felt electricity crackle and pop throughout her clenched cunt, his cock igniting the explosions with every gliding stroke. She felt like she could hardly breathe. Time stood entirely still. After a few moments, she began to move with him, matching his rhythm with her hips.

"There we are, my love," he whispered into her ear. "Come back to me."

"Fucking breed me," she cried out, eyes squeezed

shut against the unbearable sensations ripping through her body.

Simon pumped harder, his hips slamming into hers until they began to throb from the impact. She didn't care at all. Sierra found his mouth, their tongues meeting, marrying into a delicious twist that fluttered in her stomach.

He had proven himself to her, as he had time and time before. Now that this primal need had been met, they could be one.

Sierra could feel his knot pressing against her entrance. She groaned into his shoulder in anticipation of the sweet sting of being filled far past capacity. Her body was made for this, and it screamed for him to deal the final blow.

"Please, Simon, oh, please," she whimpered, near tears. "I need your knot. I fucking need it, please."

His hips began moving more erratically, gasps and groans coming in short bursts, and then it happened. With one final thrust, he popped his knot inside of her, and they both threw their heads back and lost themselves entirely.

The climax poured over them like a sheet of ice water, shocking her entire system so thoroughly that she almost felt like she would begin seizing. Her jaw was slack, but no sound came out of her mouth.

And then, the weight of her entirety came crashing back into her body. She hadn't even realized she'd been floating just above herself until the fall came. Sierra felt like blacking out, but she held on.

The best part was coming.

SIMON

Once his knot was in place, Simon rolled them gingerly so that they were lying on their sides. Facing each other, he could stare deep into her hazel eyes, stroke her cheek, and enjoy the rush of every feel-good chemical his brain chemistry had to offer.

This abject bliss was low and burning. They could feel the tender tug of that intimate connection with even the slightest movement from either of them.

"I love you," Simon whispered, finally nose-to-nose with his bitch.

"I love you, too," she responded, voice still raspy with the remnants of desire.

Realizing she wasn't satisfied, his left hand traced a line down her waist, over her hip, and then curved down to slip a finger between her glistening thighs. She whined in response and lifted her right leg only slightly, straining against the knot.

Simon began circling and squeezing, bringing her closer and closer still to her peak. As they stayed tied together, he would do so again and again, until he was free to fuck her once more.

For now, the wolf was satisfied… but that would only last for so long.

Gunsmoke & Mirrors

Something strange is afoot. Things have gone missing, windows have been opened... and Alicia is ready to face off against the culprit.

PAIRING:

MF

KINKS INCLUDED:

Gun Play, Exhibitionism,
Public Sex, Noncon/Dubcon, Stalking

SPICE LEVEL:

5/10

CHARACTERS:

Alicia, Alistair

Somebody had snatched her panties from the gym locker room on her lunch break. Alicia wasn't sure who it was, but she would absolutely be at the police station after work. Strange things had been happening lately: possessions disappearing, moving, windows opening by themselves. Alicia was certain somebody was breaking into her apartment and fucking with her. There was no other explanation.

Right now, that was neither here nor there. She was about to present to the entire board, and her pussy was bare to the world. It didn't embarrass her. Instead, she felt a roiling rage inside of her, higher and higher with every passing moment. Alicia was pissed that somebody would do this to her. The fact that any man would violate her space and take her intimates made her blood simmer.

They had been part of a set, as well. She had worn her best lingerie today to bolster her confidence. It was pouring salt on an already festering wound, and she felt like hissing and spitting from the irritation like a pissed-off cat.

Whoever it was, they'd better hope that the cops found them before she did. Alicia had been raised by a Navy SEAL, and she was not fucking around when it came to self-defense. She knew her way around a fight and always carried a firearm with her. The only exception was work. Guns weren't allowed on the premises, so she left hers in a secret compartment in her car in the parking garage.

The current speaker motioned to her, and she

realized he must be inviting her up. Alicia grinned, showing all of her brilliant, straight teeth, and stood gracefully from her chair. Appearances were everything. She would be damned if she let hers suffer because some sick pervert had stolen her panties.

***

The presentation went well. She had gotten incredible praise, although she was sure her boss would have critical feedback for her the next day. It was a good sign, and one that she needed. Alicia wanted to move up in the company, and the CMO was looking for a new executive assistant.

It would come with a slew of perks that she had been salivating over for months. Ever since befriending another assistant to one of the executives, she'd realized that she was working in the wrong position entirely. Alicia no longer wanted to slave away in the trenches of the social media team. No, she had her eyes set on something juicier.

And *somebody* juicier, if she was being honest.

The current CMO was a gorgeous, built man who commanded a room without question. Most assumed he was the head of the entire company until they met the actual CEO. Even his name felt regal.

Alicia wanted to lick every part of his body.

Was it a little screwy to want to sleep your way to the top? Sure. But when the opportunity to sleep with such a gorgeous specimen arose, Alicia wasn't one to turn it down. The opportunity hadn't presented itself yet, but she had no doubt it would, if her latest fantasies were anything to go by.

Once she was finished washing her hands, Alicia headed back to her desk. She had to share space with the other people in the marketing department, but she didn't mind it. She didn't crave alone time when she was working. She enjoyed collaborating with her coworkers.

Her space was heavily decorated. She had photos of her Chihuahua, Pablo, plastered all over in cute, funny frames that made most people groan. Bright pink, lavender, and white were the primary colors at her desk. They were happy and light, and she wanted to remain upbeat while she was sloughing through corporate hell.

Alicia had barely sat down when she felt somebody behind her. Spinning around in her swivel-chair, her face dropped when it was Alistair who stood behind her.

"Disappointed to see me?" His smooth, low voice was accompanied by a raised eyebrow.

Alicia faltered for a moment before responding, "Oh, no, no. You just spooked me!" Her bright smile was back, a hand held to her chest. Being in front of him never failed to fluster her.

"I was going to ask if you could stay late tonight. We need to generate content for Genevieve."

"Oh, yes, of course. I don't mind at all," Her response was breathy, and internally all she could hear was, *Shit, shit, shit, shit.*

Of course, he would ask the day she was going to go file a police report. Alistair had no idea, though. She was sure he would advise her to leave work immediately and file the report if he *was* aware. While intimidating and gruff, the man was also known to be highly protective of his team; fatherly, almost.

If only he'd let her call him Daddy.

She realized they'd been gazing at each other in silence for a few moments. There was a small smile curving his plump lips almost imperceptibly. Alicia gulped again.

"Well, I'm going to get back to it. Don't let me catch you slacking, Alicia." He winked at her before turning and walking back toward the elevator that would bring him to the executive floor. She loved how put-together he was. Alistair's locs were pulled back into a ponytail, swaying with his every step. His suit was tailor-made, hugging all the right places that made her mouth water.

To top it off, she was sure he got weekly manicures. His hands were just *too* perfect. In every way, this man was entirely out of her league.

But you couldn't stop a girl from dreaming.

*****

Alicia's feet were throbbing, and she was strangely wired. The content had taken far longer to generate than she'd thought, and it was now close to midnight. She'd had to maintain high energy during video recording, and it had bled into her off-camera attitude. It would be a while before she'd be able to sleep.

Then again, maybe not, because Alistair Dupont was walking beside her in companionable silence. He had insisted on walking her back to the parking garage, at least, since it was on the way to his apartment. Alicia's heart thumped at the fantasy that he might invite her back and what that might entail.

She knew he wouldn't, however. This was a kindness he would give to any of his employees. He was just that type of man. It made things even harder for her, because his gentle nature just made her want to fuck his eyeballs out even harder.

"So, um, I heard you're looking for an assistant..." she started, clearing her throat awkwardly and looking away from him as she shifted her bag on her shoulder.

"I am, yes." He sounded almost amused.

"Well, good luck. I'm sure you'll find somebody perfect for the position."

"I noticed you put in your application."

Alicia nearly froze. She could hear her pulse as time slowed down. She hadn't expected him to come out and say it directly.

"Uh, yeah, I did. I just thought it might be a nice change of pace. I used to be an assistant, and I liked it very much."

"I see."

He didn't say anything else and, for her, the following silence was incredibly awkward. Thankfully, they had arrived at the parking garage.

"Thanks for walking me back," she said, tucking a stray strand of hair behind her ear.

Everything stilled once again when she felt Alistair's hand pull the strand of hair back out of place. She looked over at him, lips parted, heat creeping up her neck.

"You're beautiful when you let your hair down. You should do it more often."

The way he said it was so brusque and businesslike that she felt like he was commenting on a recent report rather than her appearance.

"Take care of yourself, Alicia. I'll see you tomorrow."

With that, he was walking away, and she was caught between being frozen in place and wanting desperately to race after him.

"Thanks. I will," she murmured to herself, raising a hand to run her fingers through the brunette locks he'd pulled loose. His touch had been so gentle. She shuddered at the memory of his fingers ghosting down the strand, barely brushing against her cheek.

Alicia was wildly distracted as she stepped off the elevator for her floor. She didn't know what was happening until a hand was over her mouth and a gun was pressed under her chin. She let loose a yelp, but quickly extinguished it at the threat of being shot. She didn't dare thrash or scream. Her heart was racing so fast that it physically hurt.

Furious tears leaked out of her eyes. Alicia was hyperventilating, despite her attempts to control her breathing. Her attacker still hadn't said anything, and she was terrified of when the words would come. He pulled her further toward the back of the garage.

She wanted to fight back, to keep him from disappearing her into the shadows, but she wasn't stupid enough to think she could disarm this person. If the gun went off, it would almost certainly fire at *her*. She knew how to wrestle control back from a man. In this situation, she simply didn't have the leverage. Her knees were quaking as they kept moving, and she realized she could see less and less around her.

Finally, they came to a standstill. The hand over her mouth moved down to wrap around her neck instead. Alicia shook and whimpered.

"Tell me this much, fucker. Was it you? Did you take my fucking panties today?"

Even on shaking legs with a bladder that threatened to empty itself without permission, Alicia found her voice. She always would.

"I did, and if you keep running your mouth, that's where I'm going to put them next."

Alicia sucked in a sharp breath as she realized that it was the same voice that had been haunting her fantasies for months now.

It was Alistair.

"Are you fucking joking right now? This isn't funny!" she whispered, but it was high-pitched and carried further than she intended. Alicia's eyes darted around the cavernous room to ensure they were still alone.

Am I fucking serious? she thought to herself as she realized what she was doing. Was she seriously concerned about her *stalker* being caught?

"I assure you, Alicia, that none of this is a joke," He lowered his head, and his breath was warm and soft against her ear as he spoke. "I promise that I have been incredibly patient, but I need you, and I can't pretend I don't anymore."

Despite herself, Alicia felt her heart swell at the idea that Alistair had been pining over her just as much as she had over him. Even if it was a wildly messed up way of going about things, it was strangely sweet. Romantic, even.

But she was still pissed, and this was still dangerously close to a kidnapping.

"Well, then why don't you put the gun away, and we can go somewhere more comfortable..." she purred, pressing her ass into his upper thighs, since she was too short to hit his cock directly.

"I'm very comfortable, actually," he rumbled, low and deep.

Alicia opened her mouth again, and was rewarded by him spinning her around and placing her against the wall behind them. He seemed so careful not to hurt her with his movements, even as he pushed the gun into her mouth.

"Let's not be coy. I think you have a few secrets you wouldn't want getting out, don't you?"

Her head swam, and Alicia stifled a moan. Great. Not only was he her stalker and her boss, he was also aware of her gunplay kink. How he'd come across this information was a different story, and the tale would likely horrify her.

"Hands above your head, Alicia."

She whimpered and obeyed, eyes squeezed shut. She wasn't crying anymore. Instead, Alicia almost felt like laughing at how ridiculous the situation was.

"Let's play a game," he whispered, eyes boring into hers when she opened them. Alicia sneered in response.

"I'm going to play with that wet cunt. You're going to try not to come. If you win, I'll turn myself in. If I win, you're going to come back to my apartment."

It took Alicia a moment to realize what he was saying. Her eyes rolled back, and she mewled. It wasn't fair. This wasn't fucking *fair*. She all but growled when she felt his hand make contact with her thigh and then start creeping up toward her quivering center.

That did nothing to stop him, and within moments, she felt one of his fingers dip into her wetness.

She saw stars. Alistair had found that bundle of nerves that had swelled and grown tender from every move this man had made since pulling her into the back of the garage.

"Look at how wet you are for me. Such a good girl, getting yourself ready for my cock. I know how desperate you are for it."

Alicia groaned, closing her teeth around the barrel, which had forced her jaw painfully open. She couldn't stop the flurry of whimpers that fell out of her mouth around the cold metal filling it. Her thighs were tensing, and she could feel the walls of her pussy begin to contract.

No, no, no, she thought to herself as the climax began to build. It was all too much. Between the realization of one of her darkest fantasies, to the man delivering it, to the knowledge that this had to go *somewhere*…it was just too much. He had one finger lazily circling her clit now, but gaining speed as she bucked into it.

Alicia's head fell back as much as it could, and she let loose a howl as the climax ripped through her.

"That's my girl. Just let go. You need this, baby."

The words were whispered so tenderly, she could almost convince herself they were from a longtime lover instead of a man who had been systematically terrorizing her for weeks.

But he wasn't wrong.

She bathed in the warm, washing pleasure that cascaded through her body in every direction. It was sharp as a knife, and it cut through every defense mechanism she had been building against him since she had learned out who it was.

Both of them froze as a light appeared out in the distance.

"Anybody in here?" The booming voice was likely a security guard. She and Alistair locked eyes. It would only take one yell… one scream…

She jerked her head to the side, motioning to the corner, staying perfectly still aside from that movement. Alistair caught on immediately, and they edged over, ducking around the side and continuing until they were between the concrete square that she suspected was a supply closet, and the cement wall of the garage.

The wall stopped almost above her head. Alicia was small, something that had always been bothersome. She barely passed for five feet tall. She refused to allow the doctor to tell her what the official height on record was. She didn't even want to know.

When the light from the guard's flashlight bounced off the wall, she felt her heart leap into her throat. Alistair was holding her, the gun safely pointed toward the ground. If she wanted to, she could disarm him and alert the guard.

If she wanted to.

Instead, they huddled there together until the coast seemed to be clear, and then waited a little bit longer still. Once sure they were alone, Alistair grabbed her chin and jerked her head toward him.

"Strip for me."

Alicia blanched. She was not getting naked in

the middle of a parking garage for her fucking stalker. The last thing she needed was to get nailed for indecent exposure.

"Now, Alicia."

This time, the command was emphasized with a gun pressing into her cheek, pinning her head to the wall. She sneered at him, eyes closing to slits, and then moved her shaking fingers to the buttons of her shirt.

Alicia took her time, but her trembling would have slowed the process down regardless. She slipped her shirt off, letting it fall to the floor, thankful for the lukewarm night air. Next, she shimmied out of her skirt, which fell to her feet once it cleared her ample hips.

Before she could unclasp her bra, the gun fell from her face. Alistair was openly staring at her, mouth open, eyes dark with passion. Alicia almost gasped when he stepped forward in the cramped space, using his free hand to reach behind her and unclasp her bra.

When that final piece of clothing fell, Alicia was entirely naked. She crossed her arms and whimpered.

"No, baby, don't be embarrassed. You're fucking beautiful, and I'm going to show the entire world."

Before she could question what he meant, Alistair was picking her up and throwing her half over the wall, so she was bent over it. Alicia had to stop herself from screaming. She was up ten stories, staring down at the street below, precariously dangling with only Alistair's strong hands keeping her from slipping right over.

The height was dizzying. She felt the blood rush

to her head as she lifted her arms to try and brace them against the top of the wall. She couldn't, and so instead, she pressed them flat to the concrete in an attempt to feel any sort of security.

Without warning, Alistair's hands were back. This time, he dropped a hand over the side of the wall so he could slip it down and play with one of her nipples.

"Please, please put me back down, Alistair," she gasped. "I'm not joking. This isn't funny."

"Alicia, my love, you don't hold any of the cards here. I'm going to fuck you senseless right where you are. I want the entire world to see those beautiful tits bouncing while I pound your pretty pussy."

She could only hold back a desperate moan when she felt the head of his cock line up with her entrance. Alicia's heart was hammering, the distance to the ground becoming more and more blurred as tears gathered in her eyes.

All of it disappeared, however, when he thrust his hips forward and slid inside of her. An explosion of pleasure followed, and Alicia found herself lost in a heady rapture as he began fucking her. His long, strong strokes ravaged her needy body, which craved his touch and rewarded him with her arousal.

She could hear guttural sounds wrenching themselves out of his mouth. She imagined him, teeth gritted, eyes blazing, determined to see her fucked good and well. Alicia almost forgot that she was dangling ten stories above the ground, being ruthlessly pounded by the phantom who had haunted her every moment. And she wanted more.

What the fuck is wrong with me? was all she could think as the pressure of an orgasm built once more in her lower belly. Alicia whimpered, shifting back and forth to encourage him deeper, and then sucking in a sharp breath and regretting the movement. It made her all too aware of her predicament as her top half swung in the air.

This thought was quickly swept away as his pace increased, and all she could think about was that thick cock pushing her further and further to her peak. Alicia bit her lip hard enough to draw blood, trying her hardest not to make a sound.

There weren't people below, as far as she could see, but she wasn't taking the risk that the security guard would somehow spot them.

But when he lost control of his hips, she lost control of her vocal cords. Alicia yowled like a wild cat as the last hard pumps sank him deep inside of her pulsing walls. Her clit was grinding into the concrete, rubbing her raw but driving her to another plane of pleasure. She felt the peak of her climax rise from the depths of her lower belly, piercing every organ as it speared through her body.

And then it was over.

He pulled out of her and helped her off the wall onto her shaky feet. Alistair cupped her cheek with the hand holding the gun, and they stared at each other for a few minutes.

"This is going to make the office really awkward,"

she whispered.

"Why? Do you think everybody will know we're fucking?"

"No, Alistair. It'll be awkward because you'll be in prison, and I'll be sitting in your executive chair."

It was Alistair's turn to stifle the noises trying to escape his mouth.

"Oh, so feisty, Alicia. We'll see how bold you are after the next few hours."

"I'm going home, Alistair."

"We had a deal, Alicia."

"That doesn't–" She was cut off by him bending down and throwing her over his shoulder. He carried her the rest of the way to his car, leaving her clothing behind. She wouldn't need it where they were going.

Spellbound

Captured and humiliated, Isla has resigned herself to the fate that awaits her... whatever that might be. Soon, she'll find out that what her captors have in store is not what she thinks.

PAIRING:

MFM

KINKS INCLUDED:

Noncon, Ritual, Double Penetration,
Virgin FMC, Praise, Pet Play, Edging

SPICE LEVEL:

8/10

CHARACTERS:

Isla, Cassian, Knox

She pressed her back against the damp stone. Shadows slithered against it behind her. The only light spilled like honey across the hay-strewn floor, slow and golden. Isla had given up entirely on the hope of rescue. She'd thrown away the wishes she made, folded the fading lights into her palm, trying desperately to keep the glow alive.

In the end, the men who took her had sapped not only her will to fight but her will to *dream*, and that was so much worse.

She was draped in a simple dress made of soft cloth that didn't itch at her skin like the peasant garb she usually donned. Isla wasn't sure what they wanted, but she was certain that it would spell the end for her. She had heard the tales of women taken in the night, quaked with fear when her mother warned her not to wander with stories of ravishings and sacrifices.

Naturally, Isla never listened.

The call of the wild was a keening cry she couldn't help but investigate. She spent her days crafting flower crowns in the meadows, running her fingers over the soft, spongy moss that clung to the massive trees in the forest she called home.

Vishtar was surrounded by all the wonders nature could provide. She felt at home outside in the sunshine, a creature of the light. Here, in this darkness, there was nothing for her but misery.

She sat with her knees bent, arms wrapped around them to give her a small sense of sanctuary.

Drowning herself in darkness was far easier than facing the man sitting in the chair just next to the door. They always left somebody to watch her, no matter what, and she still hadn't adjusted to the constant company. The coolness of the floor radiated through her feet, digging deep into the skin until she couldn't feel her soles anymore.

"Isla, it's time."

With a start, she looked up to see Cassian. He was a handsome man with broad shoulders and kind eyes. She couldn't understand why he was doing this to her or allowing the others to do it.

"I beg your pardon, m'lord?" she croaked, throat dry with disuse.

"It's time for you to fulfill your destiny. Come here."

A thunderous terror boomed in her chest. It ricocheted off of her ribs and finally struck her in the heart. Isla had no idea what her *purpose* was. She only knew what she had thought up in her head during the long stretches of impenetrable silence that cloaked this prison.

She stood slowly. Every muscle shrieked in misery as she stretched out. Once upright on her shaking legs, she edged her way toward one of the lords who held her captive. His brunette hair fell in messy strands around his ears and eyes, curling at the edges. She watched with tear-filled eyes as he unlocked the door and opened it, motioning to her to follow him.

As soon as she was out, a metal collar was placed around her neck. The heavy weight of iron was not unknown at this point in her stay. They insisted on restraining her any time she left her cell, no matter the reason. It wasn't often enough for her to be used to the bite of cold metal against her neck.

Cassian leaned down, taking her chin in his hand.

"Don't fret, my pet. It will all be over soon. Now, on your hands and knees."

***

Candles lined every wall, lending a dreamlike aura to the small room where Isla was led. She crawled on all fours like a dog. It was a humiliating way to travel, and she could feel her cheeks burning brighter with every painful step. They said it was to lessen the chances of her escaping. She was convinced it was simply a way to degrade her further.

And then, she saw it.

A stone altar protruded from the center of the floor with a baroque tablecloth draped over the top. Upon that rested a knife.

Feeling faint, Isla froze, and the metal collar yanked against the back of her neck. Her palms dug into the ground as she braced herself backward against the pull of the lead.

Cassian stopped short and turned around, face set with a soft calm. He reached out a hand to gently stroke the crown of her head.

"Easy, now. It will all be over soon."

"Please…"

He paid her cries no heed, instead bending down to scoop her up into his arms. He cradled her to his chest, and she clung to him, head burrowed into the place where his shoulder met his torso. Even while he carried her to what she assumed was her death, Isla felt an odd comfort being held in such a way. It was almost as though she was safe here, in the fortress he had created just for her.

Once he stepped foot on the dais, Isla began to sob. The tears came hot and heavy, quickly soaking the man's shirt, and her fingers dug painfully into his shoulders.

She heard him heave a deep sigh, his grip on her tightening. Instead of reprimanding her or harming her, as she thought he would, Cassian instead turned and carefully sat down with her still in his grasp. Once seated, he curled himself around her, holding her close and rocking back and forth.

Her cries echoed in the small chamber. Once she began, especially now that he was showing her this kindness, Isla couldn't stop. These monsters had taken from her everything. Now, they would take her life. It wasn't fair.

"There now, my pet." She heard his voice, though it sounded distant, "You're going to be fine. We're not going to hurt you."

It was a reassurance she desperately needed,

but not one she could trust. Isla expected he would say anything to keep her calm until he drove that jeweled knife through her heart.

Isla whispered, "Then what will you do with me?"

"You'll see. But I promise, it only hurts for a moment. After that, I think you'll come to enjoy the ritual."

His cryptic words did little to soothe her stuttering heart. Isla whimpered deep in her throat, squeezing her eyes shut and wishing away this hell she had found herself in. She barely heard the whine of the opening door, not acknowledging the presence of who she assumed would be Knox.

"Is she ready?"

Knox's voice always made her want to shrink. It was cold, and there was an edge to it like steel. In a moment, it could become sharp as a sword, cutting just as deeply. She'd seen him lose his temper with the guards who had fallen asleep when they were supposed to be watching her.

"Yes. She's throwing a little bit of a tantrum, but I think we can begin."

She could hear the rumbling timbre of Knox's voice through his chest. Isla still clung to Cassian, but stole a glance at Knox when the two men began speaking again. Through her rising anxiety, she barely felt the heavy collar fall from her neck and clang to the floor, Knox freeing her from the weight.

"Get her on the slab. We need to start. The moon

is almost in alignment."

Isla began sobbing again. She felt another pair of arms reaching down and yanking her up. She gasped and began to fight, clawing at his hands and letting loose a scream she didn't know she was capable of.

"Oh, stop it," Knox growled, pinning her arms painfully behind her back.

"My pet, you need to get on the table," Cassian purred in her ear, standing to assist Knox with moving her.

The fight finally left her body, and Isla went limp. She had never been a fighter. Her place had always been the healer, the lover, the tender one with soft hands and kind words. If she were to meet her end, she decided she would do so with the same grace she lived her life with.

Once they had set her on the altar, the men took their place on either side. Cassian lifted her chin with two fingers so that she looked into his face. Her eyes, though filled with tears, locked onto his defiantly.

"My pet, do you see the moon above?"

She glanced toward the ceiling and noticed that there was an opening at the top. The moon was almost directly overhead, swollen and milky silver.

"I'm sorry to keep you in the dark, little one. The ritual won't work if you understand what's happening. You must be pure of heart and mind."

Her lower lip began trembling, followed by her entire body when Cassian picked up the knife and held it in front of her. With Knox still pinning her arms behind her, she was helpless to stop him.

When he placed the tip against her skin, she closed her eyes and waited for the pain. Instead of stabbing her, however, he pulled her dress away from her body and began slicing through the front of it. Isla's eyes flew open, and she gasped as her front was bared to him.

"Must you humiliate me before you kill me?" she cried out, snapping her legs together and pulling her knees up to cover her naked breasts.

"Oh, my pet, we aren't here to kill you. Although you will die many small deaths tonight, that much I can promise you."

She screamed when he sliced through the shoulders of the dress, hacking away until the garment fell completely from her body. Now entirely revealed, Isla wished they *would* kill her.

Do they mean to ravage me? she thought suddenly, her eyes widening. Surely, if they were going to defile her, they would have done so by now. But the signs were all there. They were holding her down and stripping her naked. There couldn't be another explanation.

"Please, no," she cried out, "I've never– I'm–" she sputtered as Cassian began prying open her knees to reveal her core. She could feel the stirrings of something in her belly, an unfamiliar sensation that made her feel somehow lighter.

"It's okay, little one," Knox whispered gently in her ear. "We won't hurt you on purpose. We need your virgin blood, or the ritual cannot be completed."

It all came together now that he spoke the words

she so feared to hear, and she gasped. Isla let out a fierce growl, kicking harder at Cassian. He dodged her attempts and wrapped his arms around her legs, pinning them to his hips. He stared down at her center, a predatory gleam shining in his dark eyes. His tongue dragged across his lips, wetting them.

"What are you doing?" she cried out when he slid forward, slipping her legs through his arms so that her legs were still being held firmly even as he came closer and closer to her pussy. When she could feel his hot breath on her skin, Isla gasped, all of her muscles contracting.

Even while she feared what he was about to do, Isla found herself distracted by the warmth pooling in her lower belly. There was a part of her now awakened that hungered for more. Isla cried out when the tip of his tongue touched her slit, dragging a wet line up until he hit the top, where his tongue burrowed through her folds.

In the next moment, she was crying out for a much different reason. A brand new sensation burst into existence between her legs when his tongue met what it was looking for. She gasped and bucked her hips, eyes opened and brow furrowed in confusion.

"What-what are you doing?"

Her words were lost in the next moan that clawed its way out of her throat. When she felt a finger prodding at her entrance, she gasped and tried to shift backwards away from the pressure.

Knox leaned forward, his lips next to her ear, and whispered, "You're doing so good for us, pet. Just relax those pretty legs and let us worship you."

The sweet words, so unlike him, brought her a measure of comfort.

The finger slipped inside of her, and Isla shut her eyes once more, adjusting to this strange feeling. When he began moving inside of her, she felt a sharp spike of pleasure spear her womb. Isla threw her head back and let out a wild cry when his tongue found that tender place once again, moving in tandem with his curling fingers.

Another finger joined, and she found herself whimpering and thrashing. This was unlike anything she had known before, a searing rapture that left her mind broken and tangled. Some sort of pressure was building. Something was *coming*, but she didn't know what. She just knew that very suddenly, she didn't want him to stop. She didn't want him ever to stop.

Cassian pulled away, and she let out a low groan, her hips bucking toward him. His face glistened with her wetness, and something inside of her stirred at the sight.

"Do you want more, my pet?" he asked, voice deep and rich with desire. Isla could feel her reddened face, the pounding between her legs rising to a pitch that drove her to madness.

She looked away, tears welling up in her eyes again. She couldn't help but feel like a common whore, being sullied by the hands of savage men who cared nothing for her but what her body could do for them. It left her feeling empty and dulled to the pleasure that still pulsed in her veins.

Knox released his hold and wrapped his arms around her chest. She recoiled at the feeling of his skin against her bare breasts, but it only pushed her deeper into his chest. His head nestled into the crook of her neck and shoulder, and he softly kissed the skin there.

"If you're a good girl, we'll let you have your pleasure."

With that, his hands unwrapped, and either one cupped a breast. Isla squirmed, her skin burning with shame as he began to roll her nipples between his fingers. She gasped and mewled as he continued working her pebbled peaks. There were too many new sensations, too much happening at once.

She breathed heavily, her chest heaving with the effort. Cassian slid up her torso so that she was trapped between the two men. She could feel the hardness between his legs pressing against her, and her heart froze at the thought of it sliding inside of her.

"Hush now," Cassian whispered against her lips, one of his hands holding the side of her face. She pressed into it, turning her head so that she could hide her face away.

"Did you like that?" This time, the voice was in her ear, Knox's hot breath tickling.

Isla gulped, opening her mouth to respond and then closing it. Tears pricked at her eyes again. She had. It had made her feel things she never had before, and that was terrifying, but the pleasure was addictive.

"Will you… Will you do it again?" She whispered,

pausing halfway through as her cheeks turned bright pink. This was as improper a situation as she could ever imagine. She would be lying to herself if she didn't feel a warmth between her legs at the thought of being ravished by two handsome men.

"No, my pet, not tonight," Cassian said, stroking the apple of her cheek with his thumb. "We have something better planned for you."

She shook her head slowly, the realization of his meaning dawning on her.

"Oh, no, I can't," she whimpered. "I'll be impure, sir. Please."

"You don't ever have to worry about those conventions tying you down again," Cassian responded, bringing his other hand up so that he was holding her face between both of them.

"You are going to stay here with us to be worshiped as the queen you are about to become, Isla."

Knox's words chilled her, casting seeds of sorrow over the fields of her heart. She was sure they would take root there and be nurtured by every pang felt when she remembered things she missed.

But why would she even want to go back?

Her life had been misery, even in the face of being kept in a dungeon. Life was hard for those who were not gently born. Isla was of the earth her family tilled, not of milk or honey or wine like the royals they bled onto the soil for.

She pushed the thoughts away. They were impure.

Cassian was undoing his britches, reaching a hand into his pants. He pulled out what Isla thought to be an impossibly long and girthy manhood. She gasped and shifted backwards, pressing herself into Knox's barrel chest. He held her tighter. Cassian pulled her toward the edge of the table while Knox pushed her forward.

She would be at risk of falling if it weren't for Cassian directly between her legs, his cock pressing into her slick folds. Isla felt tears pool in her eyes again. She sniffled pathetically and squeezed her eyes shut.

Both men moved forward, squeezing her tightly between their chests. Their heads laid on either of her shoulders, and their lips were next to her ears. Isla whimpered as they both began to whisper sweet things to her, Knox's fingers playing with her nipples once more.

Cassian put a hand between them and began pushing her open with the head of his cock. She breathed hard, quivering in anticipation.

"I promise that we will never be unkind to you, Isla," Cassian whispered. "Just relax, and you'll have your pleasure soon."

With that, he slid just the tip of his manhood into her, rocking his hips back and forth to gently work his way inside of her.

Isla bit her lip, her face scrunched. She waited for the explosion of pain she had been warned would accompany her first time. Instead, she felt a small pinch, and her eyes popped open in surprise.

Cassian was working his way deeper inside

of her. She felt him stop once he was buried to the hilt. She gasped and began shifting her hips. It was an odd sensation, to feel him inside of her, but it wasn't unpleasant. In fact, she felt an odd urgency for movement.

She wrapped her hands around his neck, leaning forward into his embrace, and moaned softly as he began to thrust his hips. The rhythmic, gentle motion made something inside of her roar with need. Isla groaned and sank her teeth into Cassian's shoulder.

The reaction was immediate and incredible. He threw his head back and let out a primal sound that ricocheted off the walls of the chamber. Isla felt a building pressure again, edging her urgency into a fervent need. She gasped and moaned as she began to shudder.

And then he slipped out of her, leaving her throbbing with something akin to pain.

"No, wait," she cried out, trying to pull him back.

"Patience," Knox barked, putting a hand around the front of her neck and pulling her back. Her head fell back into him, her throat burning from the contact with his hot skin. She knew she should be fearful, but instead, the fire in her belly blazed brighter.

"Oooh!" she moaned as his other hand reached around to play with her nipple.

"Isla, kneel on the altar. Come, let me show you."

Knox slid off the altar. They helped her into a kneeling position, and then bent her over so that she was resting on her forearms with her ass in the air. She shook and took shallow breaths. She wasn't sure where this was leading, but it was still so embarrassing to be on display in front of these men in such a way.

Knox climbed back on the table, kneeling behind her. Cassian leaned forward to kiss her cheek and hold the back of her neck tenderly. When she felt Knox parting her buttocks, she gasped and tried to sit up. With Cassian's hold on her neck, she couldn't.

"Wha–" Her sentence ended in a sharp gasp as she felt a finger prod at her rear entrance.

"Easy now, sweet one," Cassian whispered, stroking the side of her neck with his thumb as he spoke into her ear. "It's just part of the ritual. I promise it'll feel good for you too, if you let it."

Her entire body went rigid when an oiled finger slid inside of her, pushing past that tight ring of muscle working to keep it out. She buried her face into her forearms and tried to relax through it as he twisted and scissored his fingers. It burned, and she was desperate for it to stop.

Finally, he was done. He pulled his fingers from her and then pressed the head of his cock against her instead.

"It can't fit... It won't fit..." she cried out, biting her lip and sniffling as Cassian shushed and crooned at her.

Without a word, Knox pushed forward and entered her. She felt a burning, pinching sensation that was far more intense than it had been when Cassian slipped himself inside of her. When she whimpered in pain, Cassian slipped a hand underneath her and began rubbing a finger against her core. The jolt of pleasure distracted her from the impossible stretch of Knox's cock filling her ass.

Within a few moments, encouraged by Cassian whispering sweet nothings into her ear, Isla felt an aching, deep pulse radiating from where she was being slowly fucked. It wasn't unpleasant. No, in fact, it was shockingly good.

"You're doing so well for us, Isla," Cassian purred. "You were made for these cocks."

She began to buck her hips, whether to rock back onto Knox's manhood or to rub herself shamelessly into Cassian's hand, she wasn't sure. Isla cried out as a growing rapture began to take hold. It felt like something was about to snap inside of her, as though some peak would be reached.

Cassian pulled his hand away, and Knox ceased his thrusting. She gaped, turning her head to look helplessly at Cassian. He smiled and stroked the back of her cheek with a finger.

"Come now, my pet," he said, placing a hand on her sternum. "Sit up."

She wasn't sure such a thing was possible with Knox still buried inside of her. Regardless, Cassian began helping her up, keeping her angled so that Knox didn't slip from his position. Once her back was against Knox's chest, she was breathing heavily and trying to manage the feeling of fullness that threatened to take her over.

Cassian climbed onto the table. His cock was fully erect, still monstrously large, and she found herself fascinated by it. In her twenty-five years, she'd never seen such a thing. The bulbous head was purple, leading down a curving shaft to a set of… She wrinkled her nose.

That was a part of men she decided she would never like. The wrinkles were unsightly.

The distraction only held her attention for a few fleeting moments. Cassian was edging toward her on his knees, staring hungrily down at her core. She shifted on Knox's cock, making a soft noise at the sensations that flooded her pelvis.

"I'm going to fuck you now, Isla," Cassian said, holding her jaw and forcing her to look at him. He was firm but gentle.

Her eyes widened as Knox lifted her by the hips, his massive cock sliding partially out of her. Cassian positioned himself at her entrance, and then Knox started sliding her down.

She threw her head back and panted, struggling to accept both of them at the same time. It felt impossible, like she would tear in two, and Isla found herself begging them to stop. She was writhing, daring only to move in short bursts against the fullness that might rip her apart.

"I love watching you try so hard for us," Cassian whispered into her ear. Knox began lifting her a little and sliding her back down. It was a strange rhythm, akin to a dance, and she slowly began to go limp as she relaxed into it.

"There we are. Our good girl. You feel incredible. So fucking tight." Knox's harsh rumble filled her ear. She would have flushed from his crude words were it not for her whorish behavior. She was now wriggling, helping Knox slide her up their shafts, begging them to keep going.

"Are you ready?" Cassian whispered into her ear. She wasn't sure what he was referring to, but the pressure was back, and it was tenfold. She whined with the need for them. Cassian slipped his hand between them and began playing with her again, rubbing a finger against a place that made her scream with pleasure.

She threw her head back and witnessed the swollen moon. It was a glorious sight. Silver-white beams filtered through the hazy darkness of the candlelit room, casting the three of them in a glow. Isla shut her eyes to it all. She felt as though something was coming.

She heard the two of them chanting in a language she didn't know. It felt miles away from wherever she was, floating in a haze of pain and pleasure and need.

All at once, it hit her.

There was a thunderous snapping sensation, and a wave of warmth saturated every inch of her body while her pussy contracted and rippled. Isla shrieked, her body jerking as her orgasm continued. The chanting had become fast, almost urgent, and as she looked over Cassian's shoulder, she saw shadows swarming against the walls.

Perhaps earlier, she would have been frightened.

Now, she felt nothing but the cocks inside of her and the intense sensations surging through her that she had never felt before. Isla was sweating, her body shining in the gossamer lighting.

The two were shouting now. Their voices stirred within her a longing for some ancient thing, risen again to life by the words flying from the men's mouths. Isla's cries mingled with their yelling in the tiny chamber until she couldn't tell any of it apart.

It was a maelstrom of noise, and Isla was lost in the cacophony. She wrapped her arms loosely around Cassian's neck, throwing her head back on Knox's shoulder. She heard them both roar, the chanting over, and their hips jerked erratically. Finally, they emptied themselves into her.

Once they pulled out of her, Isla groaned and fell forward into Cassian's arms.

"You were beautiful, you know," Cassian said, stroking her hair. "When you came for us, I could feel that pretty pussy squeezing my cock."

She sucked in sharply, eyes closing against the building shame. She had sullied herself, ruined any prospect of marriage, and she had done so with reckless abandon, enjoying her ravishing.

"Oh, what have I done?" she sobbed, her voice cracking.

"You've done nothing wrong, my pet. You performed exactly as we needed you to."

She sniffled and looked up at him. "What did I

do? What have you done?"

"You don't need to worry about the results of our spells. Only concern yourself with helping us perform the rites. I'm sure you can do that, considering how much you enjoyed it this time."

She closed her mouth and decided against pushing further. Isla was aware that these were not good men, and they weren't doing good things. She had also decided that she didn't care. No, in fact, she could get used to this.

The evidence of their joining was running down her legs, leaking from both holes.

"Please, will you clean me up?" she whimpered, looking up at Cassian through thick lashes.

"Of course, my queen. Anything for you."

The Taming of the Fool

A man shows up where he doesn't belong... and
is quickly taught why his ilk should never venture
into these woods, where fierce women live.

PAIRING:

FFMFF

KINKS INCLUDED:

*Femdom, Slave Training, Impact Play
Torture, Noncon, Pegging, Degradation,
Humiliation, Medieval/Fantasy setting…
and more*

SPICE LEVEL:

10/10

CHARACTERS:

Isabel, Amabel, August, Gisela, Amice

The chamber was just barely lit. Stone, windowless walls crowded in on all sides. It was a small room meant to hold, to imprison. The subject of this punishment was trussed up on an oddly-shaped bench. It had rests on either side for his shins and arms, which lay comfortably even despite the restraints holding his wrists and ankles firmly in place.

A collar circled his thick neck, attached to the top of the bench and firmly clipped there. It left him very little ability to move. He was silenced by a ball gag that was heavy against his tongue and teeth.

August had ventured into these woods hoping for an easy target, a woman of the wild to bring home and tame. They were creatures of myth and legend. No man who had entered the woods to find his prize had ever returned. Still, they kept trying, lured by the idea that they alone could bring order to the orderless.

He had foolishly believed that the answer was his alone. Instead of fighting the feminine power that lived in that forbidden wood, he would succumb and submit. You simply could not rage against the nature of a place. It was enshrined in the earth under your every step. The soil was steeped with the blood of men who did not understand that you must bend or you would break.

Now, he was to find out what had befallen so many men. It seemed more and more likely that it was not death, but perhaps something much worse.

They had drugged him before dragging his limp body down into the dungeon. August's bleary eyes had burned with fatigue, but he had caught glimpses of naked bodies gleaming beneath roaring fires, unspeakable sex acts playing out in plain view—men stroking each others' cocks, others allowing their faces to be fucked like a dripping pussy.

It had felt like a dream, ethereal and desaturated, like something that unfolded during a feverish sleep. August wasn't even sure that it was happening at all. It could have simply been the intoxication taking hold and feeding him fantasies that had formed long ago.

This didn't explain the burn in his skin or the hardness of his cock, however. The two fought for his attention between his moments of contemplation. It was a cycle of fear and curiosity; the wheels in his mind turned between them until they spun so quickly that it all began to blur.

Footsteps echoed loudly against the ground; the acoustics seemed attuned to enlarging all noise. August breathed heavier, the pounding of his heart beating in time to the pulse of his throbbing cock. He could hear the approach, and then the sudden cessation of movement next to him.

He couldn't even turn to look. A dark figure stood just on the edge of his peripheral vision. Due to the gag in place, he wasn't even able to ask what was happening to him. It couldn't be anything pleasant. August was known for his height and stature, but he wasn't sure how he'd fare against torture.

"You poor thing," a female voice crooned,

drippingly sweet, "I'm so sorry you've been waiting here. We're almost ready to begin, I promise."

August felt a hand on his head, tangling gently into his hair and then stroking down to the nape of his neck, where she used her nails to scrape along his skin. Goosebumps rose and his cock twitched despite the fear that burned a slow, torturous trail up his spine.

"Such a pretty thing, aren't you?" The sweetness in her voice did nothing to comfort him. Her hands glided across his shoulders, then down to his back. For a moment, she hesitated at the small swoop between his hips, gripping the swell of flesh above his ass. Time seemed to slow while his entire body turned into a heartbeat, pounding, pulsing, burning.

Then her hands slowly moved downward and gripped either cheek.

"My, my, but don't you have such a thick, luscious ass. I wonder how you'd feel if I…" Her voice trailed off thoughtfully. August felt panic rising, electricity shocking his system to give in and run. This was impossible, however, due to his current predicament.

He felt her finger drag down the plane of one ass cheek, down toward the tight center. August threw his entire weight against his bindings, desperate to escape. He made no headway, no matter how hard he struggled.

"Easy, darling. Don't hurt yourself," the voice laughed as she began circling his tight hole. August finally thought to clench himself. This only served to draw a laugh from the woman and pull her hand in further, until the finger was almost pressing inside of him.

Roars ripped from his throat. A swelling fear slammed into his ribcage, churning waters darkened by the sickly taste of terror. *What in the name of the gods are you doing?* He cried out mentally, desperate to make his voice heard even as he knew it was hopeless. His manhood twitched, and he knew that beaded moisture collected at the tip.

It had been his goal to kneel at the feet of the women who ruled in these lands. He would have willingly prostrated himself, offering his body for their consumption, willing him to bend even as his spirit demanded their domination. Once he had one of them in his possession, he could gentle her as much as he liked.

He'd frozen, and the prodding at his asshole continued. Her other hand stroked an asscheek, and she was murmuring to him all the while.

"You're doing so wonderfully for me… Such a good boy…"

Just when he suspected that her finger would push inside that tender ring, another voice sounded off the walls.

"Gisela, stop that. You're not supposed to begin early! There's a protocol."

The new voice was higher, but not an unseemly pitch. It reminded him of birdsong.

"Oh, Isabel, you're no fun," Gisela laughed, giving his ass a squeeze. "Relax yourself, little one, so that I can remove my hand."

The shock of such a ridiculous pet name made his body slacken automatically. *Little one?* he thought incredulously. He was a mountain of a man, hardly someone who would inspire a pat on the ass and a sweet nickname.

But that was exactly what he received.

Gisela had removed her hand as promised when his body loosened. He heard her footsteps moving away from him. The blood in his veins was icing over. They began speaking, and he listened intently, desperate to glean information.

"Where are the others? Have they been gathered yet?" Gisela asked.

"They're on the way but running a little late as usual," Isabel, the newcomer, responded.

"Well, how unfortunate. Do you know how long they might be? I'm anxious to begin. This one has such a nice build. That plump ass will melt beneath my hands once we break him in."

"Don't get ahead of yourself, Gisela. The poor thing is already so nervous."

"Let's step into the hallway, shall we? I think a few minutes alone might do him well."

August still had the self-respect to feel a burning anger at how they referred to him, almost as though he were a frightened animal. If it weren't for the restraints, he would grab them both by the neck and show them how much of a man he was.

His throbbing cock hung through a hole. He was

terrified of why that might be the case. It was still erect. Despite himself, August began fantasizing about pinning the mysterious Gisela to the floor and ripping away her clothes. He'd pry her legs apart, swat away her hands, and plunge deep into her sweet cunt…

The daydream was interrupted by the sound of feet filing into the chamber.

"Get some more light in here, please, Amabel," Gisela's voice rang out, clear and assertive. August was beginning to suspect she was in charge of whatever was taking place.

"Yes, my lady," a soft voice whispered, leaving an audible trail like a fading ghost.

A woman stepped out into his field of vision, and he finally could see who had taken him captive. His heart nearly stopped at the sight of her. Not from her beauty, although that was indescribable, but from what she wore… and it was not in admiration, but in horror.

There were straps around her hips and thighs, leading to a harness system. A large, curving manhood jutted out from between her thighs. August had never seen anything like it. What she planned to do with this fake cock, he had no idea, but creeping suspicion made his stomach bubble with fear.

He assumed this was Amabel lighting candles a few feet in front of him. Her golden hair was swept up into an elegant plait hanging down to the small of her back. She wore leather trousers and a jerkin over her white undershirt. He noticed the flat, black paddle hanging from her belt, as well as a knife tucked into her tall riding boots.

August quickly tried to deduce whether anything there could help him escape. If he could somehow loosen his restraints or convince them to let him free, he could certainly overpower them and take the knife. From there, it would be easy to hold a hostage and negotiate his freedom.

It seemed that the spirit of masculinity would have to see him through, which stood in opposition to what he had assumed. In the meantime, while he waited to make his move, he evened out his breathing and concentrated on listening closely to the conversation around him.

The women had spread out, but they were standing around him in a triangle, one behind him and the other two on either side.

"Did you travel well, Amice?" Gisela asked.

"Oh, yes, wonderfully so. It was lovely to take the boys out for a nice, long go in the carriage. They try so hard for me! I seldom have to raise the whip. You simply must join me soon!"

This new voice was raspy, her vowels slightly elongated, words coming at her leisure. They were moving on before he could wrap his head around her confusing statement.

"Have we put any thought into what this magnificent creature might be suited for?"

"Oh, I think he should be kept in direct service.

We won't really know until he's fully trained, though, will we?"

"No, I suppose not. But Amabel has finished up with the lighting, so I think we can put him through his paces."

The voices ceased, and instead there was a strange tension in the room. All of the women began to come into view. He tried to match each voice to a face. To his growing horror, all of them wore the same harness. Each seemed to have a different shape, girth, and length. The largest, the one that made his mouth dry and his heart stammer, belonged to the woman he was sure was Gisela.

She stood tall, easily close to his height, with raven-black hair that fell in giant, loose curls around her shoulders and breasts. Unlike the others, she was naked aside from the harness. He could see the dense patch of hair between her legs, and the toned, lean thighs that would normally spark his desire.

Now, he felt nothing but numb. August closed his eyes and took a shuddering breath.

"Hello, little one."

The voice was close enough to startle him. He jerked, and his eyes shot open to see Gisela leaning in close. A hand cupped his cheek and he felt the brush of a thumb moving back and forth. The gesture did nothing to comfort him.

"I suppose you must be wondering what all of this is," she began, voice steady and warm. "Well, you were stupid enough to venture into our home. We don't care for men in our midst. That is, men whom we do not keep solely for our pleasure. You have become one such man. We'll spend however long it takes to gentle and train you before assigning you to a role in our ranks. Your behavior and willingness to please will determine where we place you."

Her hand dropped from his face, and August stared into her deep eyes, desperate to find a trace of the tenderness her gentle sex was known for. He saw nothing but the gleam of a predator who knew she would soon eat her fill.

Without another word, she stood, her breasts level with his face. The nipples were peaking, and he yearned to lean forward and twirl his tongue around the stiff point. His cock was still throbbing beneath him. He was all too aware of how exposed he was. There was a hole in the bench that it hung through, into the open air beneath him.

He was at least four feet in the air. There was nothing beneath the structure he was helplessly bound to. August began jerking against the restraints again, feeling the crushing weight of desperation deep in his bones.

They were going to violate him. Those cocks they wore were not for show. Her finger testing his reaction earlier was just the beginning. August screamed through the gag. The noise was pathetic, and it did nothing but wear him out.

He was sweating and shaking by the time he was done.

"Easy now," Amabel laughed, running her hand through his hair. "It's going to be okay. There, there."

Her gentle comforting did nothing to negate his rising panic.

"Alright. I'm going to put that beautiful, plump ass to use." Gisela's voice again. "It might pinch a little at first. Just do your best to relax through it."

August began frantically thrashing once more. He stopped, eyes wide as saucers, when he felt an impact strike him from behind.

Sharp pain finally overcame the shock and he realized that, yes, a hard hand was whacking his buttocks over and over. He could feel his ass was rippling with the effort. He began crying out at each sharp hit despite himself, desperate to make it stop. His face burned bright with shame and humiliation.

Until now, he hadn't registered how exposed he felt, or how mortifying this entire situation was. Now, August could feel his body burn brightly hot. The spanking stopped and he could hear Gisela panting slightly, likely tired from the effort.

"You are to behave yourself, pet," she managed through deep breaths, "or you're going to have a very sore bottom to show for it."

Her wording set his neck on fire, the blush of his face creeping down toward his chest. Her tone was patronizing, as though he were a new servant who needed to be reminded of their place. It was not uncommon, after all, for corporal punishment to be used on househands.

August himself had struck one or two especially mouthy servants of his own.

Now, he thought perhaps he had been too quick to raise a hand.

Something cool poured onto the very top of his ass, and he felt it seeping down into the valley between his cheeks. His heart was erratic, and a hand slipped through his now-slick asscheeks, even as he clamped them shut.

"It's no use, love," Gisela said, in gentle exasperation. "We have this liquid made for us by our magic users. It makes you impossibly slick, and we can part through these cute little cheeks like butter."

She used her other hand to squeeze his left cheek softly. He screeched in fury, lips curling back to expose his teeth. He wanted to grab this fucking bitch by her throat and show her what power looked like. If she truly wielded authority, she would let him free and they could see who came out on top.

He felt a finger prod at the tight entrance once more, and he whimpered—a pathetic, terrible sound.

"Oh, dear," Gisela sighed. "Amice, Amabel, could you two comfort the poor thing through it?"

"Absolutely."

"Oh, my, yes!"

There was a flurry of movement, and Amabel leaned over into his view.

"This is going to help," she said, presenting a vial filled with a sloshing, red liquid.

She popped the stopper out, and then she cupped

his chin and held his head still. With the other hand, she tipped the vial into his mouth between his right cheek and the gag in his mouth. He had no choice but to swallow or choke. The drink tasted mostly of nothing, with a faint sweetness lingering once it had slid down his throat.

"That's also courtesy of our magic wielders. It'll keep that pretty cock hard and help you understand how good this can feel if you let it. It's for our entertainment and pleasure in the end, but it can also feel good for you."

Her words chilled him, even as his skin tingled with the heat of indignation.

In the next moment, he felt a different sort of tingle settle over his skin. This was the growing heat of arousal, a need which had gotten under his skin and seeping into his bloodstream. August groaned, his cock painfully enlarged, straining against the hole that was now just barely too small.

"Here, this will make things easier," crooned Amice, who sounded strangely distant. He realized that this was because she was beneath the structure that kept him captive. A slick hand moved up and down his shaft, the same liquid they had poured on his ass was now coating his cock.

August moaned deeply. Warmth gathered in his tightening balls. It felt better than any pussy he'd fucked. He was sure this was what ascension to the heavens would feel like.

He was so enraptured with the treatment his manhood was receiving, he almost didn't recognize the press of something against his tight back entrance. August gasped when it pushed inside of him. The tight ring of muscle protecting him pinched and burned at the invasion. Then, he felt a *snap,* and only an echo of the pain remained.

He shifted, gasping for air as he came to terms with this invasion. This wasn't supposed to happen to strapping, powerful men.

The thought of it made his own cock throb harder. Fantasies he kept deeply hidden began playing in his mind–being bent over a table, being taken by a towering woman who would dominate him entirely, being sucked off by a faceless man while another played with his nipples, and yet another fucked August's pathetic, desperate mouth.

But that was his private sanctuary of filth, a testament to something so wrong inside of him that he was convinced heaven had never been an option. In these fantasies, he was willing. Here, in this balmy dungeon, he was unable to defend himself against the intentions of these women.

August wasn't yet used to the sensation of his ass being filled when Amice ceased her movements. His cock felt like it had swollen to an impossible size; he was certain it would be bright purple at the head. Despite himself, he whimpered, a pitiful sound he didn't mean to make.

"That's okay, sweet one," Amabel said, sounding genuinely sorry. "You're being such a good boy for us. You barely even fought your first plug."

His nostrils flared, eyes bulging at her bright, loving tone. How dare she speak to him in such a manner? He wanted to rip open her bodice and take her as violently as he had ever taken a bitch. She'd bleed between the legs for days when he was through with her.

The violent thought was interrupted by two fingers between his asscheeks again. He was certain it was Gisela who was pulling and pushing on whatever was lodged inside him. The sensation liquified his insides and made him choke out a groan. He felt whatever it was pop out of him with a hard tug. He cried out again, this time in pain.

"Hush, now, it wasn't that bad," Gisela chided, slapping his ass. "You're being so dramatic. Such a silly little thing." She was once more speaking to him in that chiding, patronizing tone that made his hackles raise.

Then, something much larger laid against the small of his back. He began hyperventilating, trying his best to shake his head from side to side.

Oh, no, please, he thought desperately.

"Amice, if you would," Gisela said, and he could feel her hands working the false phallus, coating it in that slick liquid that was covering his ass and thighs in a sticky glaze. She pulled the cock back and he felt the head of it slide between his cheeks, coming to rest against his asshole.

Before he could wrap his head around what was happening, his manhood was covered by something warm and wet, pleasure exploding through his torso. It was a mouth sucking gently, a tongue swirling around his shaft. August's mind was immediately pulled to what was happening beneath him.

Even so, he sucked in a breath when he felt Gisela push her hips forward into his ass, and her cock slid inside of him. Amabel stroked his face, whispering praise into his ear, while Amice continued licking and sucking.

"Are they normally so docile at first?" a new voice asked, bright with curiosity.

"Not usually, no. He seems to be taking to it fairly well."

Gisela was gripping a hip with one hand and rubbing one of his asscheeks with the other. She didn't move forward, allowing him to adjust to the cock lodged inside of him. After a few moments, she snapped her hips back, yanking the phallus back out of him, then pressed it forward, slowly sinking back inside.

He was torn between the new sensations. August knew his body was betraying him; desire had pooled between his hips until it was full to brimming. He fought hard, even while his blood sang for the wet mouth wrapped around his manhood, the humiliating feel of hands on his waist while he was being mercilessly violated.

Then, something happened. Chilling pleasure ripped through him, a heat that ate away at his resolve and made him squeal out a pathetic moan. Gisela laughed, and he groaned in response, still processing what he had just felt.

"I think I just found his sweet spot," she sang,

squeezing his hips sharply and then wiggling her own back and forth, her cock prodding into something inside of him that made his toes curl.

Again and again, she drove her hips at such an angle that bright lights erupted in his vision, his eyes crossing and then squeezing shut entirely. August couldn't control his whimpering and whining, and he knew he would be begging for more if his mouth wasn't full. The liquid they had poured down his throat was now coursing through his veins. That had to be why he was so lost in a haze of erotic longing when he should be plotting the death of every woman in that room.

The stroking and thrusting stopped in the same instant. Gisela pulled slowly out of him and Amica stopped her ministrations. Sweat was pouring off of his body in sheets, making him slide, if only slightly, on the leather bench.

"Well, that was delightful. Who wants to go next?"

His heart nearly stopped. *Next?*

Amabel was still stroking his cheek, her face pressed against the curve of his neck.

"You're so lucky. That tight little ass is going to get fucked so thoroughly tonight. Just imagine how good it's going to be once we let you come!"

August was trembling, beads of sweat collecting on his forehead, terror taking hold of his racing mind. She couldn't possibly mean… all of them? Was one not enough? Did they crave his misery and shame so much that they had to drag out his domination until he broke entirely?

Still, his ass throbbed, and he knew it was from the need to be filled once more, even as he shunned the thought.

He felt somebody new take their place behind him. His eyes squeezed shut. He begged for mercy and, underneath his pride and ego, he begged for more.

Happily Ever After, After All

After his extensive training, August becomes accustomed to his new life as a toy for his Mistresses. However, there is a newcomer who may shake things up.

PAIRING:

MM

KINKS INCLUDED:

Dubcon, Ass Play, Oral

SPICE LEVEL:

5/10

CHARACTERS:

August, Murdok

Three weeks had passed, including one escape attempt that had ended in a horrifying punishment. The unique discipline he was experiencing in this vibrant castle was enough to make the most shameless harlot blush. August had come to accept his fate. He did whatever was asked of him quickly and obediently. They had gentled him entirely.

Today, it pleased his mistress that he should be present for a visitor, a merchant who was bringing her exotic treasures. Fruits, jewels, books, and clothing were all presented to her discerning eyes. Gisela had decided to keep him for herself, collaring him once she had broken his spirit.

The process had been grueling for him. She seemed to take a special glee in humiliating and breaking him.

He wore nothing, his engorged cock on display, balls tight with need. Inside of him, a large plug readied his ass for what would come next.

"While we talk about pricing, would it not be appropriate for your pet to warm my lap?" The merchant was a broad-shouldered man, dwarfing August, even though he himself was considered tall. The man's thick thighs were spread slightly, and he could see the evidence of hardening in the form of a thick outline.

August gulped, feeling his heart drop at the realization that this man would likely fuck his ass tender before the night was over. That was, if he was lucky. If the merchant was particularly deviant, it could lead down dark alleys that would mean nothing but trouble for August. He remembered a specific night, before he had fully accepted Gisela as his mistress, when he had been tied down, his ass spread so an entire table of visitors could stare at the tight little hole they'd be welcome to use as they pleased after dinner.

His cock twitched in response to the memory. He had never come harder than that night, or as often. They had introduced him to the concept of explosive, internal orgasms that could be repeated time and time again, even as his body cried out from the usage.

There were clamps on both his nipples, though they were there for decoration and not painful. A gold chain hung between the clamps, falling to his lower belly where the two combined into one, leading down to a cock ring sitting at the base of his manhood. It would prevent him from coming out of turn, regardless of how they pleasured his body.

Reaching the peak of his pleasure without permission resulted in, as Gisela would put it, a very sore bottom.

"I think that would be lovely," Gisela responded to the merchant, snapping August from his thoughts. She ruffled his hair, tipping his chin up and looking into his eyes.

"Go and be good for my friend."

He pushed himself forward, crawling on all fours to the merchant, keeping his eyes on the floor. Once he was next to his legs, he felt the man bend, his strong hands grasping August's full hips. He gasped as he was lifted, turned so that his back was against the other man's chest. The man wrapped his hands around his lower thighs, pressed his knees upward, and August slid down, ass on full display.

The man put a hand between August's legs so he could reach the plug sitting heavy in his ass. With strong fingers, he gave the base a few tugs, earning a few plaintive whimpers from August. All he could do was hope for mercy, even as he knew that torment was coming. His body trembled in anticipation.

Without a word, the man popped the plug out and threw it to the ground. He flipped August around so that his knees were on either side of the merchant's hips, spreading him almost painfully.

"Stay there," the man said, leaning forward to capture August's lips. His cock twitched as his mouth moved to the rhythm the merchant set, opening instinctively when he felt a tongue press against his lips. Their tongues slid against each other, August's timid while the merchant's was strong and dominating.

He could feel hands beneath his balls, fumbling with the belt holding the merchant's pants closed. August whimpered when the kiss was broken, and the merchant pressed August's face into his neck.

"Hush, now," he whispered into August's ear, kissing his temple. "I know that tight little ass is begging for my cock. You want to be fucked like a bitch so desperately. I bet you'd come for me in seconds if I threw you over this chair and pounded you as hard as I could."

As his cock began throbbing, August panted. The cock ring seemed far tighter now, constricting his manhood as it grew in response to the merchant's dirty words. August had tried to fight at first, but in the end, he had been swept up by something he had wanted all along.

It had never occurred to him that his darkest fantasies would become his permanent reality.

"Here we are." The roughened whisper wrapped around his neck, leaving him gasping for air. August tried to relax as the man gripped his waist and began lowering him onto the giant, girthy manhood that had sprung out of his pants. It was perhaps the largest thing he had ever had inside of him, and Gisela took special interest in testing the limits of how much he could take.

August drew in deep breaths, head thrown backward, eyes squeezed shut. The head of the merchant's cock was inside of him now, pushing past that ring of muscle that always made him squirm in discomfort. It hurt, and August tried to lift himself.

"Oh, no you don't," the man said, wrapping his arms around August's waist and holding him in place. "Take it like a good boy. It'll fit. You can take it. I know you can."

Whining and wriggling, August gripped the merchant's hands with his own until his knuckles were white. He wasn't necessarily struggling against the grip, but he wasn't making it easy. He was just so big. August was genuinely unsure if he could take him.

The merchant shifted August up and down, sliding a little deeper every time, and he cried out every time he was pulled back.

"Please, oh, I can't," August sobbed. "You're too big."

The merchant paid no attention to his pleading, rocking him a little more quickly and sliding yet deeper. August gasped as a bright, flaring pleasure filled his belly. The merchant chuckled.

"There we are," he purred into August's ear, rough beard rubbing against his neck. August could barely hear him, lost in trying to accept the massive cock that felt like it was ripping him in two. His mouth hung open and his arms were folded over the merchant's, holding on for dear life.

"Just relax. You'll adjust to me."

August's mouth snapped shut, though he still made noises in the back of his throat. As he squirmed and panted, the merchant began talking to Gisela about the different types of marble they could import.

It would be a long, long conversation, and August knew he would be expected to warm this merchant's cock the entire time. He yearned for a hand or a warm, wet mouth to relieve his arousal. The size of the merchant's cock meant his sweet spot was thoroughly stimulated. August desperately wanted to be fucked, just perhaps not by the incredible manhood currently stretching him to his breaking point.

Just as soon as he'd had the thought, August felt

a beefy hand wrap around his cock. It stroked him slowly, dragging up and down the shaft, rubbing a thumb over the head roughly every now and then. August let out a shrill, gasping noise he wasn't sure he had ever made before.

For what felt like hours, he sat there on the man's lap, occasionally being rocked when either his or the merchant's cock started going flaccid. August was not allowed to go soft when he was serving his mistress. His cock was to be ready at all times to receive or give pleasure.

"Well, that solves that," the merchant said with a finality. "We can go over the price of silks tomorrow. I'd like to put this poor thing out of his misery. He's practically jumping out of his skin to be bent over that table and used."

"Oh, he loves having his ass fucked. I love setting him up and watching the others line up to fill him. Watching it drip down his thighs once he's overfull… it's just delightful."

August felt a familiar rush of shame and desire. He still felt thoroughly humiliated every time she called for his service, which was daily. Gisela seemed to feed off of his degradation. He had only cried twice, but both times, she had made an example of him.

He was lifted off the merchant's still-hard cock and placed on the floor. August knelt beside the chair, rigid and apprehensive. The merchant stood, picking up a golden chain from the table and latching it to the collar around his neck. Obediently, August followed.

***

Steam was thick in the evening air, making August feel heady and fatigued. He'd been thoroughly used by the merchant, who he learned was Murdok. Currently, he lay in the man's arms, lackadaisical and listless. Murdok used a cloth to gently wipe at his back and arms, holding August close to his chest.

The water, throwing wisps of white as it met the coolness of the night, was the perfect temperature to laze in as they basked in the glow of their climaxes. Both had screamed and moaned until their throats were raw with exertion. August had been the first to break, spilling himself onto Murdok's belly as he rode him to completion.

He shivered at the memory. It was such a fresh thing, his ass still sore from the pounding, and yet it felt so distant. As he mused on the past versus the present, Murdok began squeezing him tight. August's face was nestled in the crook of Murdok's neck, his arms folded in against the man's chest. It was a comfortable, vulnerable position.

August had become well-acquainted with being comfortable and vulnerable. If there was one thing his time with these women had taught him, it was that there was beauty in the act of submission. He had learned to give himself to them entirely, letting go of any problems or worries he might have, and allow things to be taken care of by those better suited to deal with them.

There was freedom in this submission.

He looked up, eyes plaintive and searching, watching the handsome planes of Murdok's impassive face. The merchant seemed to be basking in the afterglow of his pleasure. His thick lashes lay lax against his high cheekbones. Briefly, August wished he would open those beautiful, deep eyes and return the longing gaze.

And then, he did just that, as though bidden by August's thoughts alone.

"What brought you to this place?" Murdok murmured, brushing the tip of a finger against the apple of August's cheek.

"I was a fool with more brains in his cock than his head," he sighed. August nuzzled into the merchant's neck, letting his body melt into the strength surrounding him.

"And now? Are you still a fool?"

Instead of answering, August strained his neck to nibble on Murdok's earlobe. The merchant sucked in a sharp breath and tightened his hands on August's hips.

"Only whenever there's a hard cock pressed into my backside."

Murdok snorted softly. It was true—his thick manhood was once more standing stiff, pressing into the cleft of August's ass. He whimpered pathetically in response to Murdok shifting his hips. Even while he was still sore from the night's activities, August could not deny that a low flame still flickered frantically in his lower belly.

Ever since he had learned that he could come repeatedly without spilling his seed, August had been addicted.

His lips brushed against Murdok's neck, teeth scraping the delicate skin next to his Adam's apple. In response, the merchant groaned and reached a hand between them, stroking his hand along August's quickly swelling manhood. The motion made his body go taut, mouth hanging open as the simple pleasure of the merchant's hands worked him back into a frenzy.

August had been thoroughly used. Even so, he hadn't been allowed the ultimate pleasure; to spill his seed. It was reserved for special treats and occasions when he had pleased his mistress. He prayed to every god he knew that this merchant would allow him such a glorious gift. His balls were tight and aching with the need.

"On your back now, pet," Murdok said, gently flipping them over so that August could feel the stone siding of the pool press against his shoulders. Expectantly, he pulled back his legs so that his ass was bared for the merchant to enter as he wanted. Murdok plucked the oil from the ledge and coated his fingers.

His stomach fluttered in anticipation.

Murdok slipped two fingers inside August's willing ass, scissoring and twisting to ready him. It wouldn't take long. August was already primed for entry. Instead of slipping his cock between August's plump cheeks, however, the merchant leaned his head down and took his cock deep into his mouth.

August gasped, hands flying back to hold onto the ledge behind him. Stuttering gasps fell from his gaping mouth. The cockring was still there, stemming the tide of his passion, but he felt immediate relief once Murdok unclasped the ring and threw it off into the water.

The merchant's fingers never left their place, still crooking upwards to slam into that sensitive spot deep within him. August groaned as his hips bucked erratically, unsure of whether to drive himself down onto the man's fingers or thrust his cock deeper down his throat.

When he felt his peak approaching, August cried out, begging the merchant to let him come. Murdok responded by stopping altogether, leaving August a whimpering, writhing mess. His fingers still inside of August, Murdok looked up and flashed a devilish grin.

"Do you want more?" he purred, eyes glinting as he slowly massaged August's sweet spot.

"Please, sir, please…" His mewling was answered by the merchant's mouth sliding down his cock once more, taking him fully into his throat. August watched in rapture as Murdok bobbed his head, sucking in as he pulled back, setting off eruptions of potent pleasure through his lower half.

"Tell me you'll be mine," Murdok growled, taking a break from his work. "Tell me that you'll leave this place and be my fucktoy for the rest of time."

August gaped at the merchant, eyes wide, unsure how to respond. He didn't have to think long, because the merchant ducked his head down and began pleasuring him once more.

And then, once more, he stopped and growled through bared teeth, "Tell me that you're mine, the gods be damned. Tell me that you'll leave this place with me in the morning."

"Yes! Oh, yes! Whatever you would like, so long as you let me come down your throat." His voice was strained, eyes still trained on the plump lips that he so longed to kiss once more.

The merchant dove back into his ministrations. August could feel his slick, warm mouth, so soft and gentle, combined with his prodding, pushing fingers…

It was altogether too much.

With a roar, August threw his head back, splashing into the water but barely feeling the impact. His cock pulsed with each jet of hot come, right into Murdok's mouth. The sensation was incredible. It was intoxicating.

"Oh, please, stop," he cried out as Murdok began pressing more intently into that pleasurable point inside of him.

Murdok ignored him for a moment, and then pulled away entirely. August watched through slitted eyes as he pushed off the bottom of the pool to glide over to the edge next to him. Murdok lifted a wine glass and swished the liquid in his mouth before swallowing.

"Come to me," the merchant purred once he had set his drink down, arms open.

August sighed into the man's chest, once more

nuzzling into his body. Murdok held him in a tight embrace, one hand trailing twirling designs on his back with nimble fingers.

"You're mine now, August," he whispered into his ear. "I'm going to tell Gisele that I'm taking you with me."

"I'm happy here, you know," August murmured in response.

"You'll be happier with me."

August couldn't argue the point. Every moment that passed, Murdok felt less and less like a stranger from a faraway land, and more like a home in human form. He wanted nothing more than to ride that thick cock to climax again and again.

"Rest now, my pet," Murdok said, hugging him tight. "I'll dry you and put you to bed."

With that permission, August sighed gently and relaxed into the embrace, his eyes slipping shut.

Thank You

For Reading

About the Author

Junie is a woman in her early 30s from the frigid but beautiful Northeast region of the USA. She lives with her husband, sister, and roo many animals. You can find her running The Red Fox Creative when she isn't writing.

Want to see more of Junie? Find her shitposting on Threads or check her IG for updates on all the latest.

JuniperHartmann.com

@JuniperHartmann

Acknowledgements

First and foremost, I have to thank my husband for all of the incredible support he's provided me during this journey into being an author. Without him, none of this would be possible.

Lex, Cassie, The Twins (Taylor & Taylor), and many more have all been invaluable members of my hype team. They've kept me going even when the going got tough. For that, I am forever grataeful. I am absolutely nothing without the people and readers in my corner.

This book was lovingly crafted from top to bottom by me, from the cover to the interior design. However, there is one part I couldn't do alone: editing. I give all credit to her for the readability of this collection. Without her help, it would have been an absolute mess.

And, of course, to you, the reader. Thank you always for choosing to pick up MY book out of all the options on your shelf or in the store. I am consistently honored and humbled by those who do so.

Other Books

Check out Junie's breakthrough debut, *Run, Rabbit, Run,*
and all of her other books, by visiting the QR code below.

JuniperHartmann.com

@JuniperHartmann

Praise from
Early Readers

I have said it before and I will say it again,
Hartmann can write anything she puts her mind
to and she exceeds every time.

Darkness and Spice is an anthology, which states
at the beginning of each chapter the level of spice,
pairings, and content. It has stories that will appeal
to a wide variety of spice lovers. I loved how each
story was a quick read, but it still packed a punch
that left me wanting and craving more!

Chelsea Armstrong

Darkness and Spice is a collection of nine short stories ranging from mild to holy cow! in terms of heat and kink. While each story is erotic fiction, Hartmann gives glimpses into each character's inner life and occasionally into a larger world where they live.

If this is your introduction to Juniper's work, it will have you clicking "purchase" on the rest of her books.

Kay Zempel

I loved all of these short stories! Whether you read kink/erotica on the reg, or you're just trying something new, there's a story in here for you!

Each collection states the kink level, what kind of pairing, and content warnings so you know exactly what you're getting into, which I absolutely love.

Shelby Seal

www.ingramcontent.com/pod-product-compliance
Lightning Source LLC
Chambersburg PA
CBHW032308310726
48973CB00008B/2569